I0610954

THE TROUBLE WITH A VALENTINE'S COWBOY

Texas Matchmakers At It Again, Book Three

DEBRA CLOPTON

THE TROUBLE WITH A VALENTINE'S COWBOY
Copyright © 2024 Debra Clopton Parks

This book is a work of fiction. Names and characters are of the author's imagination or are used fictitiously. Any resemblance to an actual person, living or dead, is entirely coincidental.

No part of this publication may be reproduced, distributed or transmitted in any form or by any means, including photocopying, recording, or other electronic or mechanical methods, without the prior written permission of the publisher, except in the case of brief quotations embodied in critical reviews and certain other noncommercial uses permitted by copyright law. For permission requests, please contact the author through her website: www.debracloptonbooks.com.

The Trouble With A Valentine's Cowboy

Determined and recovering, Lana Valentine is a walking, talking miracle who is still overcoming the leftover lingering odd effects of her brain illness. However, despite worry from her family, she's now determined to follow her dreams on her own terms. *Not* shielded by the sweet but overprotective love she's been wrapped in since a small spot in her brain almost stole her life.

And so, in her beloved ancient Jeep, she's set out on her own, having accepted a part-time job in Mule Hollow, Texas. She promised her family she would only take a low-stress job while continuing her writing—the gift from God that has helped her make a remarkable recovery.

She's not ready for her own love story, but is determined to finish the love story she'd started writing—the one that had helped give her a new shot at life.

Love—Jeb Denton isn't looking for it yet. He's from the famous Denton family singers in Branson, Missouri, and like his cousin Ross, Jeb walked away from the show. Now, working on Ross's ranch in this little town with the pink hair salon and other colorful buildings, he's liking his life—until he almost runs over a pink Jeep at sunrise and meets the beautiful, slightly unusual Lana.

And his life starts overturning—capsizing—toppling, much like the unusual fumbling way the new lady in town often speaks.

The woman draws him like a mug—a *bug* in a rug and he's all tangled up with everything about her. Fumbling words and all.

Fumbling isn't what the Matchmakin' Posse does; they spot a possible match and zero in so everyone can watch Jeb and Lana's roller coaster ride to love that will make you laugh and cheer as love happens in the most wonderful way.

CHAPTER ONE

The soft pink sun was just peaking over the top of Mule Hollow, Texas, as Lana Valentine, heart thundering, drove her rustic pink Jeep onto the almost vacant Main Street. She was here.

Here and ready to proceed with her life's journey.

She'd been given a gift of life, a do-over, and she was working hard to get it right. She was determined.

Driven to make the most out of this new life she'd been blessed with—and she was going to start here in this town that inspired her.

This town was famous for the Matchmakin' Posse and the hair salon owner Lacy Brown Matlock. Together, their matchmaking skills were well-known, but that wasn't what brought Lana here. Yes, after all these years, matchmaking was still going strong, but it was the town itself, the people, the strength of love, friendship, and a bond with people who cared for each other that brought her here. Of course, she had her family who loved her so much. But she wanted—*needed* to find her own independence.

Needed to lean on herself and feel the freedom…and know that she could make it on her own, especially now.

She breathed in deep, letting the soft breeze brush her skin. Her gaze was drawn to the pink building down the road as the sunlight highlighted it. Heavenly Inspiration Hair Salon made her smile. It was just as bright as her Jeep—a coincidence that she loved. Her grandmother had also loved pink and this had been her Jeep, and now it was Lana's cherished ride.

She couldn't wait to meet Lacy Brown Matlock and the new stylist in town, Izzy Cranberry Asher. Their names made her smile. Everyone included their maiden names along with their married names when they spoke about them. And yes, people spoke about them because of the sensational articles written by Molly Popp—Lana paused her thoughts, unable to remember the great cowboy Molly married and her new last name. These days Lana couldn't remember a lot of names, but that didn't make a difference when thinking about Molly's articles. They were the ongoing stories of Mule Hollow, coming alive for everyone. Because of those many articles over the course of eight years, women were still coming to town looking for their cowboy.

Not exactly why Lana was here, but—okay, she could admit—if it felt right, she might think about a match with the right cowboy. But probably not. Because for now—well, she might repeatedly get his name messed up, something she was trying hard to overcome, but mostly because she was working on her dream and finding herself, recovering from her illness in her own time, at her own pace.

She was here to learn on her own to be happy no matter what life threw at her—or slammed at her. God had given her more time on earth, and she knew that wasn't what everyone got. Because of that she couldn't waste time.

Happiness for her was a chosen way of life and she

was never going to think otherwise.

Yes, her family was worried about her, but after what she'd lived through and the walking miracle that she was—well, they'd understood and let her go without too much uproar.

They'd realized they didn't have a choice. It was her way or no way, to be frank. When she'd come out of her "downfall", she'd known it was time to do what she'd been wanting to do for a very long time. Time to take an adventure and test the waters on her own.

The time for shutting herself off was gone. The time for not living her life under the protection of her family was gone. She was on her own now. And she was determined to love it and live it on her own for at least a little while.

But she wasn't looking for a man. She'd let God be in control of that. Right now, she was just working on getting…getting her words, thoughts, and reactions in order. Simple things that she'd once taken for granted. Things everyone took for granted, but she now knew just how blessed she'd always been.

So, she was here, in a well-chosen place, to find her

own way. To rebuild her brain as much as possible and be satisfied with the way it was now. If stumbling words and name loss were the worst, she would learn to live with it and make the most of it. She was determined to use her recovering brain the right way now that she had been blessed to see another day.

She now knew and understood fully that her mind was a gift from God.

And a man—well, she'd dreamed of finding a man to love, to have children with, and to grow old with. But time had flown and was still flying away from her. Time had almost been taken from her. So, for now, still standing and determined, man or no man, she was going to live her life her way—*God's* way. And she was going to enjoy it.

When she told her family what she was doing, it had been hard on them, but they knew she was serious.

She'd been given a new chance to live life and she was doing it on her own, here in Mule Hollow, Texas. Lana was starting from scratch—and her overprotective dad had realized he had to let her.

* * *

The sun was rising as Jeb Denton drove his black Ford truck toward Mule Hollow. He was more than ready for a hot cup of Sam's coffee at the diner. He hadn't slept much after performing in the Mule Hollow Big Barn Theater show last night on his cousin's ranch. His cousin's wife, Sugar Rae Denton, had started the show a few years ago with Ross's help.

When Jeb moved to Mule Hollow, he'd walked off the family entertainment stage in Branson, Missouri. He'd walked away, weary of being on the stage and hadn't intended to get back on ever again.

He wanted to be a cowboy and had come here six months ago to go to work with Ross on his ranch. He loved the change, working hard, learning everything there was about ranching, enjoying himself like never before, and only singing when he was alone and wanted to sing.

It had been great being out of the spotlight of the family show, which had included singing all night long since he was four years old. He was loving his new life, but then Ross got trampled by an angry bull. Thank the Lord he was doing well despite having several broken ribs. But not well enough for the already booked shows last night and tonight. Or the two nights in two weeks. Hopefully for the shows after those, Ross would be healed and ready to reclaim his role.

Jeb had stepped into the spot, but only because he loved Ross and his wife Sugar Rae, and they'd given him hope for a new life. One not on the stage. But sweet Sugar Rae had a way about her, and the show showcased her beautiful acting and voice. She had the ability to help others with a dream for the stage or to just step out and try something new.

Sugar Rae's love for the show was also a ministry and she used her amazing talent four nights a month to bring newcomers to Mule Hollow.

Some talented male singers from Mule Hollow had been hired on for background and chorus roles. They were easy parts, not a lot of rehearsal needed, just a fun thing to do. They loved singing in the show and on Sunday mornings in the church choir, but they also enjoyed their lives and had no plans to be one of the main characters in the show.

That meant Sugar Rae needed someone who could handle the spotlight on the stage. And so, Jeb was back in the light for a little while, but like Sugar Rae said, "God's timing is always right whether we like it or not."

There was nothing really conniving about what she said when she asked him to get back on the stage. And he couldn't turn her down because he had been given this opportunity to come here and start a new life, which he was loving. Therefore, Jeb didn't hesitate when Ross needed him to stand in on the show.

He had had a week before the show to prepare and he'd worked hard learning all the songs, singing while working cattle, riding through the pastures on his horse, and any other time he could. He came from a family of entertainers. They entertained every night of the week in Branson, so he knew exactly what to do to get ready for last night's show. And surprisingly, he'd actually enjoyed it but hadn't slept much after leaving the barn theater.

Before the sun rose, he'd headed to town for coffee

and breakfast at Sam's and to see what old Applegate Thornton and Stanley Orr thought about the show. Those two old guys still helped out at the theater two nights a month, ushering people in and making sure everything was going okay. They might be old, but they knew their business. Applegate didn't hear well— though that was disputed whether it was true or not. Nobody could prove it one way or another. All Jeb knew for sure was that hearing aids could be turned on or off and he had a feeling that Applegate used that switch when he felt like it.

He reached town just as the darkness was lifting and as he turned onto Main Street. At the end of town, he looked over at the old house that Adela Ledbetter Green had made into an apartment building. It was huge but pretty in an historic way, with its rounded towers on both ends and long porches with rocking chairs. He looked back at the street and slammed on his brakes. There was a pink, topless Jeep sitting right in the middle of Main Street.

Tires screeching, his truck came to an abrupt halt, barely missing the pink, large wheeled, ancient Jeep.

Breathing hard, thankful he hadn't hit it, he looked around for the driver. Standing in the soft daylight glaring at him was the most beautiful, brown-headed beauty he had ever seen. He blinked. Her hands were on her hips, her eyes glaring as she strode furiously toward him.

He pushed open his door, angry himself, despite being thunderstruck by the woman.

Glaring at him, she grabbed the door he was pushing and yanked it open the rest of the way. "What are you doing?"

Out of the truck he waved a hand toward her Jeep. "Trying not to run into your Jeep that's sitting in the middle of the road."

Jeb was six feet two inches tall and the woman at about five foot nine had to tilt her head to glower at him.

Or glow—the woman was something. Her flowing brown hair flopped to one shoulder as she mimicked him and waved her hand toward her Jeep. He couldn't look away, their gazes locked.

"I—I was…" she said, faltering.

He couldn't look away as the glow of the rising

sunlight lit her emerald eyes, which were flared wide. Jeb had never felt the fire that shot though him in that moment. *Whoa, back up, dude. Get your head on straight.*

"You're blocking the road," he managed, holding his voice steady, though inside he wasn't steady. He was blown away. He readjusted his words. "Look," he said, his gaze following her hand as it dropped to her hip. He yanked his gaze back up and fought off letting his eyes do anything but stare into those flashing green eyes. "I was coming into town, and I glanced away for a moment, not expecting anyone else to be up this early. *Especially* parked in the middle of Main Street. You're the one in the wrong spot, so why are you angry? Will your Jeep not start?" he asked, even though it was clearly running.

"No." She sighed, letting her gaze falter. "Thank you for stopping in time. I shouldn't have stopped in the middle of the road when I arrived. But it was my first time to see the town and the rising sun was amazing. I just reacted, stomped on the brakes, hopped out and took in the view." She crunched her brows and her eyes looked conflicted, then more firmly said, "I wasn't thinking. Thank you for reaching, I mean *reacting,* right away."

He was stunned. "You're welcome. Is something bothering you?"

"No, just, that it's my grandmother's special Jeep that I inherited. I usually take extremely great care of it, so I don't know what I was thinking. You could have rammed into it because I mingled—*messed* up my…" She stopped mid-sentence, her jaw locking, her beautiful eyes dimming.

His gaze was drawn to the jawline and saw it throbbing like she was gritting her teeth. Maybe in frustration. Obviously, she loved her ancient Jeep. It *was* cool looking but that was beside the point. "Don't be so angry, nothing is wrong with the Jeep or me, thank goodness."

She rammed her long fingers through her wavy hair, turning her now flashing eyes to him. "It's—" Her words halted as she heaved, or tried to heave in a breath. Her hand went to her chest and she gasped. Her jaw dropped and she tried again.

She couldn't breathe. Alarm raked through him as she bent forward, slapped her hands to her knees, and heaved in deep breaths. Or fought for breaths. It was hard to tell.

It happened in the blink of an eye, startling him then instantly concerning him. "What's wrong? Are you okay?" Instinctively, Jeb reached for her.

She waved his hand away as she remained bent over. "I'm fine... Just... I can't..." She sucked in another breath. "When I get excited, it happens," she managed before struggling for more air.

Despite her waving his hand away, he now placed his palm on her back and his other hand around her shoulder to steady her. He felt her back ribs rise hard then relax as he gently patted her back ribs. "Come on," he urged gently as if talking to a panicked person. "Just breathe slowly. Ease it in and then ease it out like you're doing."

Jeb had seen this in show business a lot. New, excited actors or singers got a little too nervous and hyperventilated, unable to catch their breath their first night. "There you go, breathe in slowly, think of something calming. Come on, you can do it," he said gently, slowly. Thank goodness she was listening, sucking air in slowly, then letting it ease out. She'd kept her palms locked on her bent knees, her hair hanging across her face as she stared at the ground.

"In and out," he repeated slowly, and she did as he asked. He had a feeling from the look she'd given him earlier that falling would embarrass her, so he was glad she was getting better and still standing.

Gently he continued rubbing her between the shoulders. "You're doing good. Steadier than you were. Now, how about I take your arm and help you straighten up so we can get you the four steps back to your Jeep?"

She nodded and turned her head to look at him through the separating dark waves of hair hanging between them. "Thanks."

He felt floored by the emotions raging inside of him just from her expressions and those eyes. "I'm glad to help. Glad you're speaking to me after the way I spoke to you." He regretted his attitude very much.

"I wasn't any better." She gave him a hitch of her lips.

He hitched his lips too, in reply to hers. "We both lived. Now, let's get you over to your Jeep." This time, the moment he touched her, awareness exploded through him like an electric force.

He'd sensed it the moment he'd seen her, and met her gaze. But this, being close to her and that hint of a smile before he touched her while she wasn't in an emergency situation, took him to another level. He was attracted to her.

There was no way to deny it. It was more than attraction. From the moment they met, everything about her infatuated him. Drew him to her ,and he didn't even know her name.

"Okay, slide into the seat," Jeb said, needing to stop focusing on how she affected him. As she eased into the Jeep, her eyes held his, sending his insides reeling even more. His fingers itched to slide along her skin. The longing danced through his arm, up to his shoulder, then tingled all the way through him.

What was going on?

"Thank you, I'm steady as a bee—I mean as can be."

He smiled. "A bee is pretty steady."

She nodded. "I guess so. I'm fine so I'll get out of the middle of the road."

"Well, if you're okay, then I need to look out because you were wanting to attack me before you hyperventilated. So, I'm really glad you're better and not able to kick me."

"I wouldn't kick you." She laughed.

"I'm not so sure about that. You looked pretty aggravated when you yanked my door open."

She was looking more relaxed, and he liked it. She propped her boots on the edge of her Jeep doorframe and cocked an elbow on the steering wheel. All she needed was a straw cowboy hat, he thought when his gaze landed on the one in the passenger seat.

Jeb grinned at the cowgirl. "I'm glad I was able to help you."

She widened those beautiful eyes that now glistened in the sunlight. "Thank the good Lord, you were able to avoid the collision that could have happened because I was stopped here in the middle of the road." She held her hand up. "Where I shouldn't have been. I'm thankful you were able to hit the brakes and not slam into my Jeep. I love my Jeep."

Looking into her eyes, he couldn't help but grin. "You love this Jeep, huh? Well, it's a pretty *pink* Jeep. I don't know that I've ever seen a Jeep this color or rugged looking. Nor did I ever think, well, never mind."

"You never thought that a girl would drive a Jeep like this. It is rugged, old, and a dream come true for me."

Okay, those words kind of stunned him. *A dream come true*? "Is that what this Jeep is for you?"

She nodded, now breathing normally. "It is. I can drive this pink ride with my hair flying in the wind or roll the canvas top out and avoid rain or cold weather. And these big wheels allow me to take my ride anywhere. They're not monster truck wheels, but they do their job. I just hadn't imagined the possibility of them getting smashed when I'd parked the Jeep in the middle of the road and a huge truck came flying up behind me." She grinned.

He just stood there. The woman had a way.

And he wasn't sure what to do about it.

Just then another big ranch truck turned onto the road, and moved around Jeb's truck and the Jeep. Clint Matlock grinned out his open window. "You two might need to take this conversation to a more private place." Then he kept driving down the road before he pulled into a space at the sheriff's office where his friends worked. Clint, Sheriff Brady Cannon, and Deputy Zane Cantrell were some of the original cowboys to get hitched and start the Texas Matchmakers or Mule Hollow Matchmakin' legend. The Matchmakin' Posse put the town on the map.

"I guess he's right," the pretty lady said, interrupting his thoughts. "We better move.

"Right. This road is about to get busy from both ends coming for breakfast at Sam's. Hey, before we go, what's your name?" He needed to know and saw her hesitation.

"How about you go first," she replied.

He grinned. "Jeb Denton. And yours?"

She hesitated again. "Lana... Lana Valentine."

Valentine. The name rang loud and clear, spurring more curiosity from Jeb.

Was she one of *the* Valentines?

CHAPTER TWO

Lana had known this would come. It always did, there was no way out and the look on his face told her it registered instantly. Cowboys knew the name Valentine.

Before he could ask her if she was one of *the* Valentines, she put her Jeep in gear, thankful it was still running. "I'm moving out of the middle of the road and heading to Sam's Diner for breakfast. Thanks." Then she pressed the gas.

The few short yards to the slanted parking space was too quick as she heard Jeb's truck door slam, his engine roar, then instantly he pulled into the parking space beside her. Heart palpitating, she shut her engine off and hopped out of the Jeep at the same instant he rounded the front of his truck. They met at the plank sidewalk. She stepped up onto the wooden walk at the same time he stepped forward and they bumped into each other. She needed out of his space; she knew it for sure when she looked up at him and her heart stumbled again.

She shoved the shocking reactions to the man away, knowing questions were coming. In the cowboy community, everyone knew her dad's spurs. She came from a very well-known name in the cowboy world.

She didn't want to admit to belonging just yet, mostly because she didn't want to make a mistake and have it get back to her dad and mom. They were worried enough about her.

By Jeb's expression it was obvious he'd heard the name but thankfully he didn't go there. "Come on, its checker time."

Relief filled her. "Is that Applegate Thornton and Stanley Orr there in the window?" Lana hoped to take the focus off her name, and the two older men were staring out the window at them.

"Yep, that's them. Come on and I'll introduce you

to them and to Sam, the owner. I came to watch them play their game while I have a cup of coffee."

"That sounds great. I had a long drive so I'm ready for a cup of Sam's black coffee. Not that I've ever had it before, but like his tough handshake is well-known, so is his coffee by everyone who reads Molly's articles."

"Yep." He laughed. "All true. Sam might be a smaller, older guy, but the man has a grip that could take down the toughest of the tough."

She laughed, having heard that before. Jeb pushed the door open and held it for her. Lana moved past him, her shoulder brushing his chest, sending a wave of warmth racing through her. *What was up with this?*

She'd noticed his touch when she'd been hyperventilating and that hadn't helped her get her breath back. Thankfully his calm voice had gotten through or she might now be laid out in the middle of the road where they'd met.

She glanced at him. Jeb was looking at her and she instantly moved forward, fully aware of the cowboy. Aware of him *too much*. She forced herself to focus on the diner, and instantly she halted.

Goodness gracious, it was everything she heard it to be, read it to be, hoped it would be. Yes, it was old, but shiny. The rustic wooden tables were cleaned and inviting. The walls were rugged wood, and the floor was clean. The ancient hardwood that had been there for who knows how long was well taken care of. Lana smiled as her gaze went around the empty diner, paused on the ancient jukebox in the corner, then settled on the two men sitting at the window. She, Jeb, and these two were the only customers in the diner.

The two men were sitting across from each other. Applegate was tall, skinny, and grumpy looking, his lean face so stern as he looked at her that she wanted to make him smile. Stanley, about the same age, was plumper, balding, but had a welcoming look on his face too.

When Lana's gaze locked with Stanley, he grinned. "App, I think we have a new lady in town. And an early bird like us. You got your hear'n aids turned on, don't ya?" He looked at Applegate.

"Yep," Applegate almost yelled. "As loud as I can stand it, to hear you talkin' to me."

She almost laughed at their exchange and the way

they talked. It was just as spunky and tart as Molly had portrayed in her writeups. Her gaze shifted to the side and caught the grin on Jeb's face as if he was watching her reaction to the checker players.

He stepped forward. "Fellas, this is Lana, and she just drove into town, as you saw through the window."

"Yup, we saw y'all in the middle of the road," Applegate said, spitting a sunflower seed at the spittoon sitting at his feet. The seed hit the rim and rang out as he laughed. "We thought you two might suddenly throw your arms around each other and run away together before you helped her get back to her Jeep."

Stanley was grinning broadly too.

"What?" she gasped. They'd thought she and Jeb should run off together—

"Don't mind them. Welcome to my diner," the short-in-stature owner said as he strode up to her with a bowlegged walk.

Sam held his hand out for a shake and she almost laughed. Instead, without hesitating, she placed her hand in his and she squeezed hard. She had a dad who'd taught her that a handshake showed a man's strength and a woman needed to give what she could.

But that wasn't why she squeezed back with all her strength. No, she knew as legend went, that little Sam had a handshake like no other, an iron grip he was known for. A test of a person, so she met his iron grip with her own—not that hers was stronger, but she'd learned to hang on for a long time. She'd been one tough cowgirl before her brain ignited. But as she joined her iron grip with Sam's, she was determined to regain her strength too and so they squeezed.

Instantly Sam's lips spread wide, and his eyes flared. "Well, alright then, welcome to Mule Hollow. *You,* little lady, are one tough cookie. And I mean tough."

That had everyone laughing. Lana was pleased that he'd given her that compliment.

"Nice to meet you, Sam," she said. "You too, Applegate and Stanley."

Sam then looked at Jeb. "It's obvious she's familiar with all of us wrinkled old guys. Did this here cowboy tell you who we are, or have you been reading Molly's articles? *Or* did you two know each other before he almost ran over you out there?"

"That was my fault for stopping in the middle of the road," she said. "And no, until that moment we'd never met."

Humor lit up his whole face. "Well, you know I'm Sam, but I don't know your name."

"Lana," she said, omitting her last name like Jeb had done with the checker players, but she then added, "Valentine," because they would know eventually.

Sam hitched a brow. "Valentine, *the* Valentine family who makes the Valentine spurs?"

"Yes." Just as she'd known it would, her name identified her instantly to people who knew spurs. "That's my dad. And my sister and her husband are in the business too."

Her glance caught the raised bushy brow of Applegate and the small grin of Stanley. And before she could stop herself, her gaze went to the handsome cowboy.

He was standing there with his hands on his hips, his head cocked to the side. "So, you *are* a member of *the* Valentine family. I wondered but didn't press."

She sighed. There was that look she always got

when people found out she was from the family of the amazing spur maker. Or those who implied she was a piece of candy with her last name.

Frustration rushed through her as she stuffed a hand on her hip. "Yes, I'm a Valentine. But I'm not a piece of candy. I don't come in a box for Valentine's Day." She slapped her hand to her heart. "I'm the daughter, but I stand on my own two feet." At least she used too. "I'm here in Mule Hollow of my own acorn—I mean accord," she corrected instantly, realizing her mistake.

She caught all the men exchanging glances and she wondered what they were thinking. Hopefully, that she was just frustrated. "Everywhere I go my name goes with me. And I get reactions." She forced a smile, telling herself to back down. "It's okay, I love my family and am proud of the business my dad has worked so hard to build." She both *loved* her mom and dad so much and she'd been helping with the business until she'd *literally* lost her mind.

Out of nowhere six months ago her brain had swelled up, took her mind away, put her into seizures and caused her to be in the hospital for almost a month.

It was a hard month for her sweet family who feared for her life with the attack of viral encephalitis. The odd and horrible illness had attacked the brain itself, not the things around the brain but a direct hit. And hers came out of nowhere and had almost stolen her life. The odder thing about it was she remembered none of those first three weeks.

Absolutely none.

Now, here she was, still struggling in many ways. But if she couldn't overcome the setbacks, she was going to live life with her oddities and be grateful for how much she'd achieved. She could live with saying odd things at the end of sentences or calling people the wrong names…and other things that sometimes happened.

She smiled as the thoughts rolled through her weary half-there brain, the brain she was so happy had come back as well as it had.

She was going to push herself so hard that, if possible, she would achieve her dreams despite what had happened. So here she was standing in Mule Hollow, Texas. Standing in Sam's Diner with *the*

Applegate Thornton, Stanley Orr, and Sam.

And Jeb, one of the many cowboys who called this place home. They were all looking at her, probably thinking she'd lost her mind just standing here looking at them. Little did they know her real reasons for being here.

She was here to recover because her resolve to be her own boss had taken over, and she was taking control of her life once more.

She and God…yes, she trusted Him. He'd gotten her this far so she couldn't not trust Him or disappoint Him. There must be a reason she was still alive. And as a result, here she stood in Sam's diner, about to take control of her life and see where it led her.

The men were all looking at her and she realized she'd stopped talking so she pushed her runaway thoughts aside and focused. She smiled at all of them, and they smiled back.

* * *

Jeb knew that the Valentines made great spurs; he even owned a pair. Jeb had worn spurs on stage in several parts of his family's show. He liked his fancy Valentine spurs, but it was obvious that Lana was tired of the recognition. He focused on her beautiful eyes and realized she looked really tired. Weary.

He touched her arm. "How about we sit down and order some coffee? We can enjoy the coffee and a meal while we watch these two fellas play checkers. And good old Sam, he'll cook you whatever you want and it'll be good. If you know about Mule Hollow, you know Sam can cook and his breakfasts are out of this world."

Relief filled her eyes and she nodded. "I have heard a lot about Sam's cooking and I can't wait to try some of his coffee and bologna—I mean bacon. Bacon, eggs, and toast with the pricky—prickly pear jelly."

Jeb caught Sam studying her too. "You'll be getting that breakfast soon," Sam said. "I'll get some coffee to you. It'll help revive you until the food is ready."

Jeb watched the owner of the diner head off at a fast pace to fetch the much-needed coffee. Jeb had noticed a few times in the short time he'd known her that Lana said the wrong word. It could be from weariness but the look in her eyes told him she'd known what she'd done and she didn't like it.

Maybe it was just that her brain was full from thinking about her move. Or maybe she was exhausted from having driven so far. Maybe she just needed a distraction.

He looked over at App and Stanley as they pretended to be caught up in the fierce game of checkers. Pretended was the key word because he knew those ears of theirs were tuned in to anything Lana said. "Fellas, who's winning this checker game?"

App gave a great scowl. "I just made a bad move, wasn't concentrating like I should. Y'all know how that is. The wrong stinkin' move happens or I say something wrong—it's aggravating." His gaze zeroed in on Jeb, an acknowledgment that he'd noticed her words. Then his gaze zipped to Lana. "You, little lady, need to get some rest today. Drive'n is rough on a person."

"Yes, it is. I packed all day getting ready for the movers, and then instead of sleeping, I started my drive. I was so excited that I couldn't help it, and here I am."

That made perfect sense.

"And we're glad we got to meet you, tired as you are," Stanley said as Sam placed coffee in front of Lana.

She instantly picked the cup up and took a sip of the hot brew. "Awesome, Sam. Exactly what I needed." She gave the old men an amazing, gentle smile.

A smile that dug deep into Jeb. So far, he liked everything about this lady. After the show and not getting much sleep last night, he also welcomed a shot of rejuvenation and took a drink of his strong, hot coffee. "Being tired is my problem today too, and Sam's coffee is what I was after when we met this morning," he said to Lana.

Sam grinned. "Great minds think alike, and I make my coffee to get people here. Okay, food will be out soon."

As he walked away App and Stanley got into a checker fight, distracting and needed. Jeb had long ago figured out that they did things like that. Distraction was a great tool and they were champions at it.

Lana loved the breakfast like Jeb knew she would. As they were finishing up, more cowboys started arriving, and the diner got busier.

"Thar's a moving truck comin' up the road," Applegate said.

"A moving truck?" Lana asked, turning to look

where App was pointing.

"Is that yours?" Stanley asked, seeing her quick attention.

"Yes, that's why I was here so early. Trying to meet, I mean beat it."

"Are you staying here in town?" Stanley asked as the truck stopped in the road just at the end of the sidewalk.

"Yes, that's why I had stopped where I did. I'd spotted my place."

Applegate put his checker down. "So, *you're* the one movin' into my granddaughter, Hailey Bell's, apartment up the stairs?"

"Yes, I am. I didn't realize who owned it. I just rented it through the real estate bureau—I mean agency."

"She doesn't always tell the renters whose place they're rent'n. But I've been wonder'n who was going to get it."

Jeb's gaze had locked on Lana as she placed her napkin on the table. "I've got to go. Can I pay you back if you cover my bill?"

"No payback needed," he said, his mind clicking.

"So, you're Hailey's new receptionist and office help for her real estate office? My cousin's wife, Sugar Rae, told me Hailey was excited to have a new receptionist."

"Yes, that's me. It's part-time and gives me time to do my other work."

"My granddaughter told me she hired new help and was excited about it," App boomed. "Y'all will get along great."

"I think so too," she said, heading toward the door. "See y'all soon."

Jeb stood up. "If you need help moving things I can help and get some others to help too."

"No, I'm good. I've got to go and let them in. Thanks, it's been fun."

And then she was gone. Once out the door, she bypassed her Jeep and headed to meet the movers. And Jeb watched her go…but wanted to follow her.

His mood, from driving into town to now, had turned around completely since meeting Lana Valentine. One look at the checker players and the grins on their wrinkled faces told him they'd noticed.

And that meant he might be in trouble.

CHAPTER THREE

Lana showed the delivery men her apartment and they were happy to get her belongings unloaded. It was early and they had a sizeable delivery several hours away in Amarillo. Lana headed up the stairs to her new apartment and unlocked the door. She stood inside and told the movers where things needed to go. The two strong men quickly carried her belongings up the stairs. Knowing the apartment was already furnished with a few things like a small couch and a bed, Lana hadn't brought a lot. Though she brought her own mattress, one she loved and knew she could get good sleep on.

But the first things the movers brought up were her large, cushioned, teal blue chair and the wide ottoman that went with it. Her kitchen supplies came next in a lot of boxes. She loved colored dishes and had a lot of them. She smiled, looking at the cute, small kitchen with its glass-fronted cabinets. Her brightly colored glass dishes would brighten up the room. Just looking at them would give her joy. The dishes would nicely offset the cream-toned couch and chair that she'd been told were in the small living room. The movers carried her mattress into the small bedroom, placed it on the heavy wooden frame, and said goodbye. Lana closed the door and looked around her new home. She thought of her dad's worry but understanding to give her the space she needed as he watched her leave.

Her dad had somehow known this was a move she had to make, plain and simple. And she loved him desperately because he'd overcome his fears for her and let her go. For that he held an even more special place in her heart than he had before…and that had been the place at the top of her heart. The place he shared with mother, who had given her heartfelt "yes" to her decision to seek her own way, but her support was always there and Lana knew it.

Now, Lana wanted to push herself with this move

and then rest. She knew all *too* well that if she didn't rest, her odd words would happen more often, like in the diner. Viral encephalitis was a strange illness, but she was learning to just laugh at the words that came out of her mouth. Especially when she was tired her mind wanted to shut down and she was working on fixing all of that by doing what she was doing…pushing herself. Pushing her limits and striving to reach into her brain and bring it fully back to focus.

But it wasn't at the moment and she knew it was something she'd thought about earlier when she realized how small Mule Hollow was. And how the cowboy in the diner with the penetrating eyes seemed to see something she didn't want him to see…could she keep her faucet brain—her *faulty* brain hidden from Jeb and the rest of the town?

Oh, how she prayed that her brain would recover to what it had been before the crazy viral encephalitis had taken hold of it when it had come out of *nowhere* to steal her life as she knew it away from her.

Her wonderful doctor, her gift from God, who'd known almost instantly what her problem was, he'd told her that they would know over time, maybe as soon as six months, how her recovery was going to be. And here she was doing great at the six-month date. Yes, the signs were good.

But not as good as she wanted.

She wrapped her arms around her waist as she stood by the window that looked out over Mule Hollow's Main Street. She was functioning on her own, and for that she was grateful. She'd taken the step to step out on her own, and she was so glad she'd come here to this town seeking what this strange illness had given her…a desire to find her own way.

So, here she was with an often muffled, *muddy, murky* brain. But she was driven with determination to *overcome* it. Or to learn to live with what God had given her. She knew it was a blessing that she was here. Standing in this room looking out over this small town and thinking more than halfway straight. Yes, the line had been a zigzag of weird recovery but here she stood. There were many out there with far greater burdens to bear so she remained grateful. And tenacious that she would achieve everything God had planned for her to achieve. He hadn't given her this gift of life without her determination to give her best effort back to Him and be grateful for whatever she achieved to honor Him in His care for her.

Just the strong thoughts sent her walking over to her huge ocean-blue chair and she sank into it, feeling the strong cushions surround her as she closed her eyes. It was time to sleep, it wasn't a complete choice but a necessity. Her brain demanded she give it some time to rest and to recover from what she'd put it through in the last twenty-four hours.

There was no denying it, it was better to sit down rather than stumble and fall. Later she'd unpack…and check out her new home. Later she would explore Mule Hollow, the place she'd driven all this way to call home.

So very much about this town called to her. And the diner had been a main draw and she'd loved it. Her next place to see—the place she couldn't wait to head over was *the* one and only Heavenly Inspirations Hair Salon. She was going to get a haircut…maybe an entire new look from the one and only Lacy Brown Matlock—or the new stylist Izzy would be fun too. She'd get her nails done by Sheri…she couldn't remember their last name but was grateful for the names that had come to her. She knew if Sheri was in town and not traveling with her legendary horse-training husband that she wanted to get her nails done too…her mind rolled with thoughts about everyone she wanted to meet in real life…not just in the articles she and the world follow…she sighed and her mind drifted as she thought of the Matchmakin' Posse. Oh, what fun those ladies were going to be…

She sighed…and her eyes shut of their own accord, and she rode the wave of hope…for what more would come.

* * *

Jeb forced himself to not follow Lana out the door. She clearly wanted to take care of her move in, and it wasn't his business anyway. So, he, App, and Stanley watched the men carry her boxes, a mattress, and a blue chair and ottoman up the stairs. It wasn't a ton of stuff, just enough to make the apartment hers for however long she planned to be here. App and Stanley went back to checkers but he'd caught sight of her standing in the window overlooking the town. Why was he so captivated by her?

He'd just met her but there was no denying that his pulse raced each time she looked at him. Or even when she wasn't looking at him but just standing there in the window looking like she was lost in deep thought.

The movers left and he'd made himself not go check on her. The woman had just moved to town, and he barely knew her. She had the right to have the day to herself unpacking or whatever she chose to do. Besides, he had errands to run and then work at the ranch so he headed toward the door. He'd come in the diner to ask App and Stanley how they'd thougth the show went last night and now that wasn't even on his mind.

But, before he walked out he went over to Sheriff Cannon, Deputy Cantrell, and Clint Matlock's table. When they'd entered the diner and headed to a table on the far side of the room—meaning they didn't want to be overheard by App and Stanley he'd understood. Sometimes it was good to get out of hearing distance from the two checker players.

Jeb walked over to the three men and they looked up at him. "I'm heading out to work the ranch. Y'all doing okay this morning?" He looked at Clint, giving him a moment to ask about this morning, trying to get a feel for what he'd thought about him and Lana blocking the road.

"We're good," Clint said. "How about you? I saw the new lady in town moving in. Thought after this morning you'd be over there helping her."

There it was. "No, I offered but she said there was no need, that the movers could get it done. And then she left. I did have breakfast with her since, as you saw, she got to town early. So I showed her where Sam's was and we got breakfast and were entertained by App and Stanley."

Deputy Zane grinned. "I'm sure App and Stanley added to the conversation."

"Yes, they did. Anyway, now I need to go get supplies, so I'll see y'all later."

"Hold up," Sheriff Brady said. "I was at the show last night making sure things went smoothly after Ross got hurt, and you did a great job. All the ladies were talking about you." He grinned. "Thought you needed to know that. The Posse has their eyes on you if you didn't already know."

"Thanks, about me doing a good job. I need to because Ross is so good; I can't let him down. And yep, I've noticed those three watching me—I could say four counting Lacy. But I think with y'alls kids she's staying busy. And that is fine with me." It was really fine with him because he wasn't sure how it would feel to be the target of the matchmakers.

Clint grinned. "She always hangs loose until the time feels right. But I have a feeling she's going to get on board the minute she sees you and that pretty, new gal in town together."

"Why do you say that?"

Sheriff Brady tilted his hat back. "We all know why, we aren't matchmakers but even we saw the way you were looking at her when we walked into the diner."

Clint grinned. "It wasn't like you weren't interested."

He knew it. He should have just headed out the door and not stopped by the table. His expression must have given him away because all three men were grinning at him. He was in trouble. If these men could see his interest there was no way Lacy and the Posse weren't going to pick up on it. And that meant he was in trouble…or did he want them involved?

The question slammed into him like a two-by-four. He'd come here for a new start but was he ready for the matchmakers or the town of Mule Hollow to be watching his every move?

"I've got to go," he said and headed for the door and knew everyone was watching him.

Sam grinned as he walked by. "Good luck."

Yep, he was about to be a target. He told App and Stanley goodbye, not missing their grins and knowing their calculating brains were working. Soon everyone in town would know that he and Lana Valentine had met.

Met this morning in the middle of the road at sunrise…and there was no telling what else would be involved in the story.

If the men in town were showing this much interest, he could only imagine what would happen when the Posse got wind of the morning's events. They'd get in on the show.

The show. He'd forgotten he had another show tonight. He realized that as he was heading out of town and then remembered he hadn't gone by Pete's Feed and Seed.

His head was messed up more than he'd realized. The supplies could wait till Monday.

He had a brain to chill out and a show to prepare for. He wanted tonight's show to be as good as last night's show. He didn't want to let Ross and Sugar Rae down. Everything else had to go on the back burner for now.

He'd been in show business all his life, so he knew when to slam the door on problems and focus.

And right now, focusing was harder than ever before because Lana Valentine was on his mind…and no amount of struggling to clear his mind of the beauty with the odd words was working.

CHAPTER FOUR

"Lana, are you in there?"

The gentle voice calling her name woke Lana from her sleep. She opened her eyes and blinked as she looked at the room…her apartment. She sat up and stretched as there was another knock on the door.

"Lana, are you okay? This is Hailey Bell."

"I'm here. Coming." She jumped up, ran her hand through her hair, hoping it wasn't crazy. Her massive dark brown, wavy curls could be a disaster in the mornings after a rough night of sleep. Her hand stilled; it wasn't night. She remembered that after arriving in Mule Hollow, she had decided—needed to take a nap. She reached the door and pulled it open as she sucked in a deep breath trying to get her brain to wake up and get out of the clouds.

"Welcome to Mule Hollow," the blonde, who had to be her new boss, Hailey Bell Sutton, said.

"Welcome!" the crowd of ladies behind her joined in.

Lana smiled. What a welcome this was. "Hello to all of you. Please, come in." She backed up to let them in. The blonde beauty entered first, followed by another smiling, vibrant blonde.

This one had bright pink fingernails that she waved as her wide smile spread across her face. "Hey, hey, hey," the peppy gal said. "I'm Lacy Brown Matlock, and like Hailey Bell said, we are so glad you're here."

Before Lana could formulate a reply, a bright pink-clad older lady with red spunky hair and a wide grin entered, grabbed her hand, and shook it vigorously. "I'm Esther Mae Wilcox and I am *so* glad to meet you."

"Now, Esther Mae, back off," demanded the frizzy gray-haired lady with a grin that spanned her plump face. She had to be Norma Sue Jenkins. "This sweet gal has to wake up, from the look of those sleepy eyes."

Lana almost gave a high-five to everyone because

she remembered Norma Sue's name. It had just come to her in an instant, giving her hope that there was more to come in name attachment in her brain.

"Norma Sue," Esther Mae declared. "I can see she's sleepy, but I can't help being happy to see the woman who drives that pink Jeep. I love the cars all you young gals drive. And motorcycles too." She grinned at the small lady with black hair in a braid who was about Lana's age and at the back of the herd beside another blonde that looked their age.

"Lee Ann Brown," she said, her brain clicked into singing the "Bad, Bad Leroy Brown" song that Molly had referenced when she wrote about Lee Ann.

"Yes, that's me," Lee Ann said, grinning. "You're hearing that crazy song, aren't you?"

She laughed. "Actually, I am. And I have to say, I have trouble with names, so it helped me." And it was true. The thought struck her. Would trying to associate names with something else, like a song, help her remember names? She focused on all the women. "I'm glad to meet all of you."

"We're glad you're here and wanted to come

welcome you," said a soft-spoken older lady with short almost-white hair. Her hair fanned gently around her face, highlighting her amazing blue eyes.

"You're A—" Lana started, unable to recall her name.

"Adela Ledbetter Green and I'm so very glad you're here." The woman's vibrant blue eyes had rested on her and seemed to see her struggling mind.

"I'm glad to be here," Lana replied and she meant it.

"We didn't want to bother you right after you moved in," Esther Mae said. "But we met for our mid-morning coffee at Sam's and heard you arrived very early along with the movers. Sam said you were more than likely taking a little nap."

"So, I held Esther Mae back," Norma Sue broke in. "And we waited till now to come welcome you."

"I was napping. I didn't sleep at all last night. I was so excited to get here." She glanced at her silver watch. "Oh, its three o'clock!" It was amazing she'd slept that long.

"Yes, it is," said the blonde who'd been standing

beside Lee Ann said. "I'm Izzy Cranberry Asher and also very pleased you're here. We wanted to invite you to the show tonight. It won't happen again for two weeks and it's wonderful. It'll be a great welcome to town."

"You'll love it," Esther Mae declared. "Sugar Rae would have invited you herself but she's getting ready for it."

The show at the Mule Hollow Big Barn Theater was something she'd heard a lot about. She was flattered that all these nice ladies were so welcoming and had invited her. And besides, she did want to go. After all, she'd actually gotten about seven solid hours of sleep. That was something that rarely happened. Yes, her brain still had to have more rest than usual, but solid sleep just wasn't normal. Bits and pieces of sleep were what she usually got.

"You'll enjoy it," Lacy added.

"I'd love to come. I've heard so much about it and…the checker players this morning said it was great. They said Jeb filled in for his cousin who is hurt."

"That's right," Esther Mae said before anyone else

had the chance. "And he's great."

"The entire show is great," Izzy said. "The cowboys all sing. I was just shocked the first time I went to a show. You see all these cowboys around here who work with cattle all day long and love it. And then lo and behold many of them can sing too."

Everyone laughed at the declaration from the grinning lady.

"It sounds great. Where do I find it? What time?"

"I'll come by and pick you up at six," Izzy declared. "It starts at six thirty, but we want to get there a little early.

"That sounds good. I'll be ready."

Everyone said a few more things about the show and her being here and how much she was going to love it. As they walked out of her apartment, Lana couldn't help but smile as she closed the door. She'd stumbled on a few things, but it seemed normal for someone new in town to not remember names. Far better than not remembering the names of those she loved. This had been a good decision. She would give her brain a workout. After all, the doctors said using it was good.

And so, she was going to do exactly that. Names, writing her first real book, and working at Hailey's office were going to help.

She moved her Jeep that had been parked in front of Sam's to the parking spot at the base of her stairs. She reached in the back and pulled out the two bags of groceries she'd brought with her. It was time to have a peanut butter sandwich—her favorite thing to eat when she didn't have a lot of time to waste. She smiled knowing the truth was it was just her favorite thing to eat and she'd inherited the love of it from her dad.

After she got back to her apartment, she made a sandwich and a cup of coffee, then walked into her bedroom and sat down on her bed to eat. She looked around the room and soon, sandwich eaten, she started unpacking her clothes from the boxes.

She needed to pick out something to wear tonight. Her motivation as she worked and thought about the show was her mind going straight to the handsome, nice cowboy. He was her draw to the show and there was no denying it.

She wanted to watch and hear Jeb sing.

No matter how many times she told herself to focus on everything else about the show, there was no blocking the truth that tonight Jeb Denton was the draw. Her draw to the show.

* * *

Jeb was stunned when he saw Ross standing backstage and as everything got finalized for the show. Thankfully everyone was making sure not to run into him with his broken ribs. Smiling and glad to see him, Jeb walked over to him. "You came tonight."

Ross studied him. "I did. I have to be careful, and it looks like everyone knows running into me would cause me pain, but I heard too many great things about your performance last night. I had to come watch you."

Jeb took his cousin's words in like they were the praise from the best. And Ross was the best. If he had left the family business and sought fame in Nashville, he'd probably have been at the top of the charts. Instead, he'd chosen to walk away from seeking fame and he'd stunned everyone by his action.

It had especially stunned Jeb. Now, his cousin's

words stunned him more. "Thanks. I'm doing my best to live up to you. I'm here for you until you can step back out onto that stage again with your beautiful wife."

Ross grinned but leaned close. "I'm looking forward to that but we have a secret that we haven't told anyone."

Something was definitely up. "What?"

"We're finally expecting again. Don't tell anyone, we're keeping it quiet for a little longer. We don't want everyone to get all excited. When Sugar lost our last baby six weeks into the pregnancy, it was so rough on both of us. But especially Sugar. It hurt her so much and she threw herself into the show to hide the pain. Finally, we decided to try again, it scared me actually. I love her so much and to see the pain she suffered was tough. I fear seeing it again, but, my prayers are for her and our baby to be part of God's plan for us. But, this time my sweet Sugar wants to keep it between us for now."

"I understand. I hated the loss for y'all." The whole family had felt the pain. That had been about three years ago and no other pregnancy had happened so this was great news. "I'll be praying. But why did you tell me?"

Ross gave him a look that dug deep. "Because she

told me how great you were last night. How perfect you were for the show."

"I'm just filling in."

"I know, but I've been thinking about backing off. And Sugar has been praying about being pregnant. And that prayer includes slowing down on the show. She wants to be a mom and maybe do a special or two in a show but not be the main draw. And I only do it because *she's* my motivation."

This was not what Jeb wanted to hear. "I know you're not telling me that you want me to step back out on that stage for good. I came here to get away."

"And I get it. I'm just letting you know where we're going—if God blesses us with a baby or if he blesses us with an adoption."

"Y'all are looking at adoption?"

He smiled. "We are. If we're blessed to have this baby, we are probably going to adopt too. It's time for a family to run around on this ranch and maybe this stage. But from my point of view, it would only be by choice. I'll never put my kid up there as an obligation. They would have to be old enough to want to be there and have the knowledge they can step away at any time."

That was it right there. Stepping away from the family gig had been hard on the family. "I get it. But Ross, I'm only back on the stage to fill in for you. I'm not going to be here full time."

"I get it. I'm just letting you know a change might be coming. Now, I'll stand here and enjoy the show. Oh, and I heard the ladies talking and Izzy is picking up Lana and bringing her for the show."

Jeb's heart did a hiccup. "She is?"

His cousin grinned. "From what I saw with the grins, I think some behind the scenes action is taking place."

Behind the scenes action? The question slammed into him as Ross chuckled. "Are you ready for the Matchmakin' Posse of Mule Hollow to get you in their sights?"

"No," he replied instantly.

Ross laughed. "Well, too late because I believe they've got you on their target board."

He'd felt this was coming. He'd made it six months off the target board. But now he'd known the moment he'd seen Lana that he was in trouble.

"Relax. If it's meant to be, it will be. If it's not, it

won't."

He stared at his entertained cousin. "It's the in-between that worries me."

"Hey, you know how a show works. Play the part then walk off the stage. Just do it all with a good but protected heart."

Jeb sighed. Those were his grandmother's words before a show. Sometimes girls would follow him or his cousins around. His grandmother had taught them that singing touched hearts and they'd have fans but keep their hearts close. He'd learned early on that she'd been right, and he'd never given in to all that crushing on him. He had decided that when he fell in love it was going to be real. That was one of the reasons he'd walked away. He knew he wanted what Ross had.

"Will do," he said. "The show will go on."

"I'm ready for it. I heard great things about last night. And the rest is up to you."

That was the conclusion he'd come to about his life. His choices. He'd walk out and greet everyone and then he'd sing the opening song.

And she'd be sitting out there.

And that thought held on with an odd longing…

CHAPTER FIVE

Lana was dressed and watching out the window for Izzy. From her spot she saw Izzy driving down Main Street in her two-seater T-bird. It was a pretty, little, sparkly mint-toned convertible, and it came down Main Street with the top down. Izzy's blonde hair wasn't really floating but it was free in the air. Lana could only imagine if she was going at a faster speed that hair would be blowing wildly in the wind.

Feeling excited, Lana headed down the stairs and reached the boardwalk as Izzy pulled the convertible to a halt. "Hey, don't you look great," Izzy said, looking up from the seat.

"Thanks." Lana hadn't really known what to wear but she'd assumed jeans, boots, and a blouse would work. If it had been colder, she'd have added one of her beloved leather jackets. She'd finally made up her mind and chosen a soft green blouse that matched her eyes and paused before shoving it back onto the rack. It had hit her that she'd wondered what he would like. *He,* as in Jeb. And that made her a little nervous, so she'd chosen the blue one.

"Hop in. We're going to have a great time. My husband, Luc, is helping park cars so you'll get to meet him and a lot more of the husbands tonight. Everyone tries to help out. We love it."

"So, everyone helps the show?" Lana asked as she sank into the low-riding seat.

"Yes, we do. It's an awesome attraction for the town." Izzy looked at her. "Wonderful people come into town and until I moved here, I hadn't realized how many people this town touches. Molly's articles about the Matchmakin' Posse and the single cowboys are well read and then this show is a huge draw too. We have a lot of big ranches surrounding us and there are a few towns within a long driving distance. But then this show came along and…wow. Sugar Rae is talented and you're going to love it. So, are you ready to go ride? Do you want the top up or down?"

Lana laughed. "Down, please. I want to ride in this car and feel the breeze."

"Now you' re talking my talk. Buckle up and let's go."

She did just that and as soon as they got out of town and the speed limit increased, the wind whipped around the windshield and surrounded Lana.

She loved it. Thank goodness she'd gotten a great sleep today and her brain wasn't a chaotic mess. When they reached the barn she felt awesome.

"Now I understand," she said, as they pulled into the parking area of the huge, beautiful red barn. It was an old barn and decorated with hanging greenery welcoming baskets of flowers and a path of red stone leading to the large entrance.

Here in the parking area the men were everywhere letting cars and busses know where to park. The barn was going to be packed it was so busy.

Then Izzy blew a kiss to a handsome cowboy who grinned as they went by. "That's my Luc."

Lana chuckled. "I had a feeling that's what the kiss meant."

Izzy laughed. "Yes, I only blow kisses at him. He's handsome but I love him for his heart and his love for me. There is nothing like that feeling between two people."

Lana took in her words and a knot formed in her gut. What would that feel like? Crazy as it was, Jeb burst into her thoughts—*Focus,* her internal voice yelled loudly as her thoughts wobbled.

Yes, she had to focus and not get sidetracked by thoughts of the handsome cowboy who was going to be singing. If she didn't focus, there was no telling what would be coming out of her mouth and she didn't want to stir the pot of trouble clamoring around in her head.

Focusing on everything around her, she saw that there were a lot of single ladies going into the barn. "So, the show pulls in single ladies too."

Izzy nodded and grinned. "Oh yeah. And I have to say, Ross and Sugar Rae are a draw but I was here last night knowing Ross wasn't going to be in the show like normal. We all came to show Jeb support because the show was changed a little bit, but goodness he didn't need our support. The dude is amazing and walked out on that stage and took over. See, it *was* a romance with love songs between Sugar Rae and Ross. But with Ross being out they changed it up and Jeb was wishing for love. And I can only say it was amazing."

"Really," Lana managed, thinking about seeing Jeb on the stage.

"You know, Ross got out of the music business because he was looking for a quieter life. And he found it. But then Sugar Rae came into town and wanted to start the show and needed his help. He fell for Sugar Rae and went back to singing because of her. But when he got hurt, they asked Jeb to step up and he did. Jeb is a great guy and I'm telling you, when he started singing last night—I've never heard a voice like his. There are all kinds of great voices, and they appeal to different people but the Denton family breeds singers. I didn't think anyone could sing better than Ross, but there is something about Jeb's voice that's going to draw a huge amount of people—single ladies, I should say, to this show."

Lana didn't say anything. She just got out of the car and watched as Izzy pushed a button to make the convertible top come up and meet the windshield.

Izzy got out smiling. "I close it because of all the bugs and snakes. I don't want to have to get in and worry about what might be under my seat."

"I don't blame you. I wouldn't want to worry about that either."

They walked inside and she was relieved that there was no more talking about singing. They were greeted by Norma Sue, Esther Mae, and Adela, who were helping set up some of the refreshments. Lana joined in and enjoyed the friendly banter.

When they ushered her inside, she was led down to a side row and about three rows from the front instead of sitting somewhere high or in the back.

Esther Mae leaned in. "Get ready for a show. I'm telling you that man can sing. And the songs… I've seen this show before. It was about two people falling in love. But they changed it since Ross is out. It's now about a little younger man longing for love and his older sister, who knows what love is and is trying to help him make the right choices. It's so heart-touching."

She looked at Esther Mae. "Do they have someone in the show he falls for?"

Esther Mae sighed. "Well, I can't tell you the ending. You'll just have to watch the show and enjoy."

Just then, the music started softly playing and Jeb strode out onto the stage. He grinned wide to the crowd and waved an arm in greeting then took his hat off and welcomed them to the show in a warm and welcoming voice like he'd done it a million times. Nothing about his welcome suggested he was a beginner. He was steadfast and confident, like he'd done it many times. When he started singing, Lana's heart began to thunder. His singing was amazing and inspiring. Somehow, someway, even in the dark, his gaze locked onto hers for a moment.

Everything inside of her went haywire. The man had a voice that filled her heart with an ache she'd never known. It was a voice full of meaning, a tone full of serenity and assurance, and as it rang through the room—the room that went quiet—it was mind-boggling how touching it was.

As she listened to the lyrics, Lana suddenly knew there was something about this man that could change her life. The thought stole her breath as she watched him sing the amazing song. The song wasn't country like she'd thought, no, she'd heard before and it had made her wonder what it would be like to be loved like that. Their eyes locked again and her heart tripped up until he pulled his gaze away to focus on everyone else in the room.

When the song ended, she was speechless. Her gaze swept the room around her, seeing what she thought she'd see—*every* woman in the audience who was looking or wishing for love believed that song was sung to them.

She had to tell herself to remember that important detail.

"I told you." Esther Mae sighed. "When that man sings, women listen."

Lana couldn't deny it, but *now* she had to listen to him sing the other songs. Thankfully all the other male singers joined into the show and the singing in the production was wonderful until the end.

But no matter how much she tried to let it go, memories of Jeb singing that first song *Start Of Something Good* by Daughtry, would not leave her brain. And for the first time since she'd nearly lost her brain, she wished she could forget how it sounded.

Oh, how she wanted something good to start in her life, but a cowboy making every woman in the room think the same thing—no, she wasn't ready for that.

But, there was no denying that his smooth, deeply touching voice sent an ache through her that she'd never felt before.

An ache for something more…

* * *

Jeb sang the opening song about never knowing when you were going to meet the one who would change your life. He forced himself to not look at the third row where Lana sat. He focused like he knew to do and sang like he always did, with heart and feeling. The song made it easy because it was a song about what he was hoping for.

Despite having just met Lana, there was a feeling he'd never felt before. When he'd lost his fight and his gaze went back to hers, the look in her eyes blew him away. Her eyes locked with his and he saw what he hoped to see in a woman's eyes one day.

The song was in the original production and hadn't needed to be changed. Sugar Rae and Ross had chosen it for the opening song because that was the hope of the show and their hope when they'd met.

He'd barely been able to see Lana in the low light, but he knew their gazes locked and held and he'd had to fight to pull his focus from her and play the room.

Play the room with his words and gaze, pulling the audience into the show. *It was a show.*

And that was his job, to pull the audience into the story…

But he knew looking at Lana there had been something more.

By the time the ending of the show came, there had been western songs of love, fun songs, and songs of hope. The main character hadn't found love by the end of the show, but it had told a story that love was out there so his character was ready, looking, and hopeful.

Just like he was.

As he walked off stage to clapping, and even the yells from some teenagers telling him they wanted to marry him, he'd had enough. This was why he'd grown weary of the spotlight.

He didn't even stop as he weaved through the backstage area and out the door. Walking in the shadows of the barn, he made it to his truck, climbed in, and drove away.

He was just singing the songs, and love wasn't as easy to find as the songs were to sing. He'd grown tired of looking in the eyes of all those ladies and knowing none of them knew him. They just loved the songs he sang with the voice God had given him that he now wasn't sure was a blessing or a curse.

He'd finally had to walk away from the superficial feelings that had plagued him in Branson. But tonight, something was different. There was a feeling in that room that had pulled his gaze to Lana. But, he had to remind himself what he'd learned in Branson, that he was a singer who never lived up to the dream his singing put in a lady's heart. Nope, nada, his songs told stories that were hard to live up to.

So, he'd come to Mule Hollow hoping to meet a woman who had never heard him sing. Never even knew he sang. A woman who'd love him for him, and not the songs he sang with the voice he'd started to hate.

But, now everyone had heard him so now what?

He felt stupid even thinking thoughts like that but it had been a hard lesson for a young teen and man to learn.

His voice, the gift from God as his family always told him, had another fault that he'd hoped to lose. But now, it was here, trailing him.

So now what?

CHAPTER SIX

On Sunday morning, Lana got up and prepared to go to church. She'd made it home from the show, heart calmed down and exhausted from the enthusiasm of the crowd.

Thank the good Lord she had remained clearheaded after realizing that Jeb had an unbelievable effect on women. It was astonishing that he wasn't a superstar. The man had the talent and the looks, but he had given it all up and come to Mule Hollow to be a regular, hardworking cowboy with no desire to be on the stage. That was what she'd heard everyone talking about after the show.

It was the talk of the night and she'd listened and kept her mouth firmly shut just in case her words didn't come out right. The last thing she needed was her crazy brain saying something she'd regret.

She admired him, because despite not liking or wanting to be on stage, Jeb was up there to help out his cousin. She respected him hugely for that but also she couldn't understand why he didn't want to use his talent.

And those thoughts had kept her up last night—these days she didn't sleep many hours anyway so that was normal. But she'd lain in bed staring up at the white ceiling of her new room as her weary mind tumbled around thinking about Jeb. And listening to him singing, he wouldn't stop his singing in her brain. And she couldn't help thinking about the way he played the audience, including her.

Played the audience. That had been a zinger when she realized the mesmerizing way his voice had pulled her in. Laying there she tried to kick him out of her brain, she'd needed sleep and so to take her mind off Jeb, she'd gone to praying. Prayers helped.

Prayers were her way of turning from worry to hope as she always asked the Lord to return her brain back to full force. But she always asked for His will to be done. And if her normal brain and right spoken words weren't to become her normal way ever again, she asked that she would learn to deal with it with His help.

While she prayed, she asked her precocious Savior to use her in any way He could. Somewhere in her prayers, she had to refocus many times to avoid unwanted thoughts, and somewhere in the midst of all of that her restless brain found peace and she slept at last.

For three hours. Three full hours instead of an hour and a half with a wake-up in between. That was her normal pattern these days. But three hours and then after laying there again, somewhere between two a.m. and six a.m. she slept again.

Sleep was important but not easy. Sleeping pills were not an option since she wasn't going to take anything to which she didn't know her reactions. She'd had nightmares from one prescription and then from another. She'd deal with the sleepless nights the way she was, and when totally exhausted, she'd sleep like yesterday when she'd first moved into this new apartment.

She got up, turned on her laptop computer, carried it to the kitchen, and made coffee. She sank down onto the chair that she considered to be her blue haven. Lana had repositioned it so she could look down Main Street. She could see the beautiful apartment that Adela had refurbished as well as Sam and Adela's smaller home beside it. She'd learned this last night after the show when she was about to leave with Izzy.

Adela had come over to her, placed her hand on Lana's forearm, and looked her in the eyes. "Not many people live on Main Street. But if you need anything, Sam and I are just down the road."

It had been so sweet, and it was as if Adela knew something was going wild in Lana's mind. And she was right, wild was the word—people with what she had had been misdiagnosed before, diagnosed with insanity. Thankfully, God had put her into the right doctor's path and he'd known almost instantly what was going on in her wild mind.

She pushed the thoughts away of what could have happened if that doctor hadn't been the one to see her.

She focused on her coffee.

Sipping her coffee, she pulled her computer into her lap, and started reading what she'd been writing. Then, she placed the coffee cup on the table and started typing the story in her mind. The touch of her fingers to the keyboard triggered the words and ideas to flow. Thoughts of where her storyline was going came to her and it was a therapy that helped.

When it was time to go to church, she walked down the stairs to her truck—her *Jeep*. She knew she was tired when even in her own thoughts she said the wrong words. That was a signal that there might be some laughter going on today. She'd learned that most times when the wrong word came out it got laughs, and that was fine—she would let it be fine. Better having fun with it rather than staying angry all the time. Counting her blessings was what she was determined to do.

What helped was getting in her Jeep, letting her hair fly in the wind like she had in Izzy's T-bird, and just enjoying the beautiful day. She'd chosen white jeans, tan boots, and a flowing peach blouse that ruffled in the wind. Izzy had given her directions to the country church,which was an easy drive. As Lana reached where the pasture ended, a small white church with a tall steeple appeared, and she smiled.

She loved it. The ride had been beautiful with the pastures full of cattle and the bluebonnets and other wild flowers growing along the road. It was peaceful—and much needed. When she saw the older church with the tall steeple, peace flowed over her.

She sighed and pulled into the parking lot then, she hopped from her Jeep feeling a new sense of energy. Smoothing her wind-blown hair, she headed toward the people gathered in groups visiting on the lawn in front of the chapel.

She'd almost reached the Posse when the grinning ladies waved her over. As she approached them, she realized though she knew their faces their names were not there today. She never knew when names would come and when they would hide.

That was the way it was these days. And she would deal with it.

"We're glad you're joining us," the pretty red head said, her grin big as she engulfed Lana in a hug. "I'm so glad I got to sit beside you last night. I told Norma Sue and Adela that you were mesmerized by the singing of that handsome cowboy over there." She had released Lana and turned her shoulders so she could see the group of cowboys talking. Her gaze landed instantly on Jeb.

Jeb, his name hadn't left her brain, and now she knew Norma Sue and Adela's names if her brain hung onto them.

"Esther Mae, let the woman go," Norma Sue demanded, unknowingly giving Lana Esther's name. "You look tired this morning. Lovely, but weary. Did you sleep?" Norma's plump face was full of concern.

"Some, but I'm used to rental—I mean restless nights." And there it was. Thank goodness the words she replaced usually had some connection to the word her brain fumbled. But many times, like now it had nothing to do with what she'd meant to say but she was able to instantly replace it with the one she'd meant to say. But not always.

If only names were that easy and sometimes nothing came. And then there were the moments mid-sentence when she lost her thought completely.

"I'm sorry you didn't sleep," Adela said. "But we're glad you're here. Maybe you can get a nap this afternoon."

"Maybe," she said as her gaze, which she'd pulled away from Jeb, now returned to him and found him looking at her. Her insides rumbled as her mind fumbled but she managed a nod as his lips lifted slightly in acknowledgment. Then, his incredible eyes brushed across her face like a cool breeze—*stop.*

"Go over and talk to him," Esther Mae said, obviously catching the look as she gave Lana a nudge with her elbow.

Lana jerked her gaze from Jeb's and met the beaming expression on the Esther Mae—*the matchmaker's* face. She'd easily set herself up for this. The thought rolled through her as she looked to each of the other ladies and saw exactly where she stood—in the target of the Posse.

Panic slammed into Lana and she wasn't sure if she could handle it all. They couldn't start thinking about setting her up. Her gaze shot back across the lawn to Jeb and he had a funny look on his face. Before she could say anything, he started walking her way.

* * *

Jeb couldn't stop his boots from walking her way. He'd known she'd be coming to the service, and he'd told himself to stay away but one look and he'd been snagged. But then, it was the next look that had him moving. The look of being lost. Her eyes had flared, then dimmed, as she looked from one Posse member to the next. Something just didn't feel right.

"Good morning, ladies. Lana, it's good to see you." He met her gaze with what he hoped was reassuring eyes.

Norma Sue slapped him on the arm. "Good to see you too, Mr. Entertainer of The Year. That was a heck of a great show you preformed last night."

"Thanks," he said, not taking his gaze off of Lana.

"Come on, ladies," Adela said. "You two have to get in the choir and I have to get to my piano."

Norma Sue grinned. "We'll let y'all talk. She's

right, *we* have to get ready to sing this morning."

Esther Mae gave him a nudge with her elbow. "Take care of our guest."

Then they walked away and left him and the flustered beauty alone.

"Happy new first day—" she said, then stopped, alarm on her face.

He couldn't help smiling at her cute words. "I like that. Sunday is the first new day of the week. You, Lana Valentine, have a unique way with words." He hoped his observation took the alarm and distress from her expression.

He'd been wondering if she didn't mean to say the words she said. That had been nagging at him from their first meeting. His thoughts rolled through the slightly off things she'd said on that day. He heard her say, "*...You could have rammed into it because I mingled—messed up my..." She had stopped mid-sentence, her jaw locking, her beautiful eyes dimming.* He remembered that clearly. Remembered how his gaze was drawn to the jawline and he saw it throbbing like she was gritting her teeth. Maybe in frustration. Now, as he watched she lifted her hand and let her fingers rub her brow. Yes, something wasn't right.

"It. Is. A…*great.* Day," she said, each word clearly thought out before she spoke them. They weren't said in a natural flow.

No, she'd made certain to get them right. What was wrong. *Nerves?* "I saw you at the show last night," he said, trying to take her focus off her mixed-up words. "Did you enjoy it?"

She dropped her hand to her side. His gaze followed and saw her fingers rub her white jeans. She took a breath. "You have an outlandish—I mean *outstanding* voice."

He knew now without doubt that she hadn't meant to say that. But he was really glad, relieved, to see that instead of looking upset, she'd lifted her chin, and her eyes had fired up as if taking the challenge, then she'd admitted to the wrong word. His heart did an applaud for her. *Way to go.*

Gently he asked, "Does that happen often, the wrong word coming out?" He went straight to the point with his question.

Lana's gaze faltered, and then she nodded. "Often," she said softly. "It's something I'm overturn—overcoming. It takes time. Will take time and strong will to overcome." Her eyes had turned determined, strong and no longer troubled.

He was overwhelmed with the news. His gut twisted. "Why is it happening?" He didn't want to stress her out.

"Because it is."

Her matter of fact words struck him hard. *Because it is*.

The service was starting and Pastor Chance Turner, a former bull rider, was ushering everyone inside. She took a step toward the church but Jeb placed a hand on her arm. "Can we talk after church?" he asked gently.

Pastor Chance had glanced at them then went on inside after everyone else as if knowing they needed a moment.

Lana looked at him, eyes wavering in the morning sunlight like water glistening. "Yes, talking, or trying to talk would be good."

And then she walked toward the church; heart

tumbling around inside his chest he fell into step beside her.

"Morn'n," Applegate boomed.

Stanley elbowed him. "Say it quietly, App. Welcome," he said barely above a whisper.

They were greeted at the door by Applegate and Stanley, who were the official ushers on Sunday morning.

"Nice to see you two," App said in a quieter but gruff voice. He waved a wrinkled hand, and the long, lean cowboy strode down the middle aisle and expected them to follow.

Halfway down the rows of pews, App halted and waved to the vacant space in the crowded church. Jeb could feel every eye in the church on them, and today it didn't feel the same as when he walked out onto the stage with his performance face on and his mind on the show. No, today his thoughts were on the woman in front of him and what was going on behind those beautiful, troubled eyes of hers.

She sat down, leaving plenty of room for him. He sat down beside her, his shoulders straight, his chin up, and a feeling of protection for this lady beside him like he'd never felt before.

She sat straight too, her gaze on the choir as Adela started playing the piano. The pastor stood and asked everyone to rise for the first song, "To God Be The Glory."

As he stood, Jeb's upper arm brushed Lana's. She shifted from one foot to the other and then, she lifted her hand to her chest, her palm opened as if handing something upward as she sang.

Her soft voice touched his heart, soft and gentle and not loud for others to hear, but as if it was just a song between her and God.

Touched, Jeb listened, unable in that moment to make a sound as her praise dug deep into his heart.

What was her story? *And how can I help her*, he prayed to the One he knew was watching.

Though they were led in another uplifting song, Jeb could not focus on what they were singing, his mind was so full of questions for Lana. When the singing was done, she sat back down beside him, her hands locked together as the preacher stepped to the pulpit and prayed.

Jeb prayed too, for guidance and for her to open up to him and tell him what was going on and if he could help her in some way.

Pastor Chance opened his Bible and began his sermon. "Today God placed on my heart the verse from Romans chapter 8 verse 28. *'And we know that in all things God works for the good of those who love him, who have been called according to his purpose.'*"

The pastor continued but Jeb locked onto those words. His gaze dropped and saw Lana's hands grasped so tightly together that it was as if she was trying to hold on. *What* was going on?

Unable to stop himself, he placed his hand on hers, and she took it, clamped onto it and his heart locked on that connection.

It was unlike anything he'd ever experienced, and he knew that no matter what happened next, it would be hard to let go of her hand.

CHAPTER SEVEN

By the time the service was over Lana had prayed many times for her words to come out right. For her to understand why this had happened to her and to move forward even if the words didn't come out right. She'd prayed for her brain and its crazy way of acting since her illness to get straight.

She knew that in the six short months, since her brain had been attacked that she *had* come a long way. She prayed that this time of stumbling on words, of words disappearing mid-sentence, and even the off-the-wall words at the end of her sentences would be things she could live with if that was God's plan. She reminded herself that coming as far as she had was a gift, and she wouldn't hide from it.

She had struggled as the words of the preacher tugged her heart. God *did* work for the good of those who love Him, she knew that from her own experience.

She'd *lived*, and yes, she had moments like just now when she faltered. In those times, He often spoke to her though someone and today it was through this verse. It was a verse she'd looked at often, a verse the Lord kept repeating to her because He knew of her forgetfulness. The last part of the verse was what she had to figure out…*who have been called according to his purpose.*

What was her purpose? That was the question ringing through her head and heart. Was there a reason she'd lived? A reason she had recovered as much as she had? Was there a purpose in her words getting jumbled up?

When the service was over, she and Jeb spoke to those who came up, those welcoming her and those telling him what an amazing performance he'd had. They were no longer holding hands, and she missed the comfort. She eased her way through the people who lingered outside, her thoughts on getting to her Jeep. Jeb eased his way beside her until they reached the gravel.

"Looks like we've made it," he said, and she heard the upbeat song from long ago by that title ring in her mind.

"Yes, we made it, and thank you." She wasn't sure what to say, but she was grateful that the words came out clear.

"Do you still want to talk?"

Did she? "Yes, I think so."

His gaze told her he was glad. "Would you like to follow me? We could run by my place and grab something to eat and then we can go to my favorite spot and talk."

She bit her lip, her insides churning as she nodded.

His eyes brightened. "Great." He walked across the gravel on the far side of the parking area, and she walked to her Jeep, got in, cranked it up, strapped on her seatbelt on and backed out of her parking space. Then she drove to the spot near the exit, something hummed inside of her, agitation—no, relief. She was going to talk. She needed to talk. Sitting there, she waited as his big, black truck eased by, turned onto the road and then he led the way.

Heart hammering against her ribcage, she breathed in the fresh air as she followed him with the fresh air washing over her, her emotions easing.

In the Jeep, her mind was free…somewhat. The somewhat came from the fact that she was about to be alone with Jeb and he wanted her to talk.

The most shocking thing was she wanted to talk.

Needed to talk.

Needed someone here to know why she might do what she might do. Might was the key word because she never knew when the oddities were coming. As the wind encircled her, that thought made her laugh. Yes, her words were sometimes shocking and not repeatable, but thank the good Lord, that hadn't happened but a few times—that she knew of. Most times it was like it had been yesterday and today.

Jeb drove past the pasture with the theater in it. A little further down the road, he turned onto a dirt road running through the same pasture. They drove over a cattle guard and she saw a small house. It was nothing fancy, more like a cabin. They parked their cars and got out.

She breathed a sigh of relief as the quietness surrounded them. "This is where you live?"

He walked to stand beside her. "Yes, this is my cabin. Sugar Rae and Ross live down the drive we passed before getting to the theater. Come on in and I'll grab some cold chicken and drinks and we can head to the river. Normally, on Sunday, I grab food for myself and head down there to fish."

She stood quietly and took in the cabin. It was rustic. "My dad has a cabin near a lake on our property. He goes there after he's been holed up in the barn with his staff making spurs. He says there's nothing that will relax you like holding a fishing pole."

Jeb grinned. "I agree." He opened the refrigerator and grabbed a bag of already packed fried chicken and tossed it into a small ice chest along with few bottles of water. Then he grabbed a bag of already prepared grapes and put them in also. "Is this enough or something you'll eat?" he asked before zipping the bag, giving her a smile.

She smiled back. "I love chicken and grapes."

"Great. There's a restroom in the guest room if you

need to take a break before we head out to the river."

"That might be a good idea." She hadn't been thinking about anything like a bathroom stop as she'd been caught up in that smile of his. And out of nowhere a song, "Oh What A Smile Can Do," played through her brain.

Her crazy brain couldn't think of names, or other words when she needed them, but it could sing to her a portion of an old song her grandmother had sung to her and her sister when they were little girls over for a visit.

In this moment, her grandma had no idea what the smile she was seeing was doing to her. Her heart, that had been struggling since church, was now dancing inside of her chest.

She spun and headed the way he'd pointed.

* * *

"It's beautiful."

"Yes, it is." Jeb smiled at Lana's words as she looked out over the flowing river that ran through his cousin's property. She'd ridden with him in the truck through the pastures to the river. It was a beautiful day, but the scenery didn't compare to the woman standing beside him. She had on boots, white jeans, and a hip length peach blouse that danced around her in the breeze.

And she took his breath away—and there was no denying it. Everything about Lana intrigued him. Drew him.

Get your brain on target. He turned and grabbed the blanket from the truck then she helped him put it on the ground near the rocky edge overlooking the flowing water. Then he set the small ice chest in the middle and they sat down.

He looked at her, wanting her to talk to him, but he also didn't want to press her. He was enjoying the time and she seemed to as well; she'd relaxed.

As he pulled the food out and handed her a paper plate he could tell she was tired, she tired easily he'd noticed.

Giving her space he didn't start the conversation with what worried him. "Ross said he and Sugar Rae had a fight with a couple of beavers around that corner over there. The beavers gnawed all his trees down and started making a dam. He had to take his land back."

"It's wild how beavers can chew trees down," she said, looking at trees.

"Even odder that they can be matchmakers, The beavers helped get Ross and Sugar Rae together, so it was amazing. Those two started out with a story our family still laughs about and they have a funny show they put on sometimes that is a takeoff from that. They had a kissin—," he stopped talking as he said the words and met her gaze at the same time. Yep, kissing her was now on his mind.

* * *

Lana couldn't look away even though she knew Jeb was about to say kissing. Her eyes had gone to his lips as he said the word and all she could think about when he stopped talking abruptly was that he'd seen her gaze go where it shouldn't have.

"So, they kissed," she blurted out, thankful she got the word right, and held her gaze steady as they stared at each other. "For the first time there with the beavers?"

"Yes." He grinned, thank goodness.

She grinned too, thankful the humor in the story rescued her. "Time to cheat—eat," she managed. *Cheating* would be getting this man to kiss her like she was suddenly wishing for.

Why did she suddenly have kissing on her mind? Because her mind was mushed and sitting there in the middle of all God's beauty with a man—with this man was mind boogying. *Boggling. Mind-boggling,* she rethought the right words, but…

Boogying with him would be fun.

She wanted to slap herself but also wanted to laugh at her thoughts.

"Is something wrong?"

To heck with it. "No, my brain got all boogied—" She clamped her lips closed and let the odd word disappear. Even though her brain had gotten it straight she still said it wrong. "I mean it gets boggled."

His expression grew serious. She'd taken this picnic from fun and enjoyable straight to her problem. "Boogying sounds fun. Do you dance?" he asked, his words obviously a try at easing her stress.

Tears filled her eyes. "I'm in a boggling time of my life. I boggle words all the time as you can see. In unexpected and the most unusual ways. Confused, baffled, crazy ways."

Food forgotten, he reached across the basket and placed his fingertips against her jaw and with his thumb he gently wiped away the tear that had escaped down her cheek. "Tell me what's made this happen. Why you look so tired all the time and fumble your words."

She took a breath, and he pulled his hand away giving her space. She missed his touch but needed the space.

"You can talk to me."

Lana stood up, needing to move if she was going to tell her story. "I didn't mean to tear up. I'm strong and don't like the tears. But I hadn't planned on letting this out either, however, it's making its presence known. Six months ago viral encephalitis tried to take me out, it rocked my brain with an infection that is still having to be overcome. It is a small spot in the left side of the brain that gets infected, then swells and I was blessed to find a doctor who almost instantly knew what I had. Now, I'm working hard to overcome the damage it did to my brain. I'm doing that but stridin—*striving* to get away from the lingering damage. But I may have to learn to live with it forever. And be grateful for how normal I am. See, the left is over the odd way things that come out of my mouth. Stopping that is not totally in my control."

"I've heard of viral encephalitis but never had any need to research it or know what exactly it is. So it's an infection that attacks a certain part of the brain?" His words were calm and helpful. Kept her on target.

She took a moment to gather her thoughts. "It is an infection of the brain—*inflammation* of the brain. It has many causes or places it can come from. Getting bit by a bug, a mosquito is one of them. Or getting an autoimmune inflammation can start it. There are many ways. But it can also come from nowhere—no known cause can be found and that is what mine was. I was normal and then, out of nowhere, I started feeling ill. Thought I had food poisoning at first but by morning, I knew that wasn't it, then thought maybe COVID. But no, by the time they got me to the hospital I was already clueless. I didn't even know my name. The high inflammation that slammed into me could have killed me."

Jeb couldn't believe what Lana was saying. "I'm so glad you survived, that you overcame it." Unable to stop himself, he took her hand. She looked unsteady, tired, so he led her back to the blanket. "Here, drink this." He handed her a bottle of water that he opened and she took a sip.

"Will it help to just talk about it? I'm a good listener."

She took another drink and her expression was stronger as she nodded. "Talking might help. But, no feeling sorry for me. I've been blessed. Sounds odd, but true."

"I believe you, and you said it without a mess up, so that says a lot."

She smiled, his insides twisted with the need to know how this crazy infection affected her.

With several starts and stops, wrong words but determination, Lana told him her story. Told him how the emergency room doctor asked her some questions. She remembered none of this but her dad stood by her side and told her what had happened. How the doctor prayed with them and said he believed she had viral encephalitis, but it would take three days to get results back. Thankfully, the doctor started her on the medicines she needed that night as they waited for the results to come back. And the doctor was right.

She was in the hospital for over three weeks, managed to speak a little, managed to basically learn to walk again in between loss of energy. She'd done it all and remembered none of it. Then she woke in the middle of the night in horrible pain that ended up being blood clots in her lungs. The pain was bad enough that it woke her brain up and brought her back to real time. And from that moment forward, she remembered.

Jeb's heart hurt for her and her family. He could only imagine the pain and fear they must have felt. He was thankful for the doctor and the medication. "I'm so thankful for your recovery. Not getting words right is nothing compared to what you lived through."

She smiled and it made his heart jump. She

resumed. "I had caring and amazing nurses and doctors. Though I don't remember all the things they did for me, my family told me so that I could thank them before they brought me home. At home, my care was also amazing. My wonderful family and friends had prayed for me and continued after I was home. My dad was my hero and was by my side constantly from the moment I was admitted to the hospital room until I came here. I can never say I'm not loved.

"I got spec—spectacular care from those who love me. And I'm thankful that now, six months later, I'm able to function pretty well. Except for the names and words that come out or don't." She placed her fingertips to the top left side of her head. "This small little spot beneath my skin controlled me, still does to some extent. I'm having to recover at my brain's pace. From the beginning I had no guarantee how much of my brain, memory, or physical actions I would get back. I've done well. But, I have a brain like a baby's, and like a baby, I require a *lot* of rest to let my mind rebuild or whatever the right word is. But I will overcome it—most of it."

He was going to look this up, read more about it and

find out how he could help her. "It's amazing. What did the doctor say helped you recover like this? Other than getting so tired and saying cute thing—misplaced words."

His words brought a beautiful smile to her lips that struck him deep. "I walk and I dictate my thoughts into a tape recorder. I've always wanted to write a book and had started one. And odd as it sounds, that has been my miracle worker. When the doctor told me I needed to slowly increase my mobility and that walking was good for me, and that television wasn't my friend because it didn't help my brain think. I told him about my walking and dictating and if that sounded like the right thing to do." Her eyes lit up and she chuckled. "You should have seen his expression. He loved it and told me walking, dictating, and then typing the words out would be a great therapy. I would be using my brain, my fingers, and legs, getting the exercise everywhere that needed it. And it has been wonderful in these short six months. My bog—biggest struggle is with names and sometimes with random words as you've heard. I never know what is going to come out of my mouth." She ran a hand through her hair and laughed. "I almost said My booger struggle just now."

Unable to help himself, he laughed and she did too.

"I just have to laugh sometimes, better to laugh than cry. See, talking to you has eased my stress up."

"It's amazing." It was. "And if that is the worst that you're left with then that sounds like a miracle."

"It is." She set the bottle beside her and looked at the grape she'd yet to eat. "Food also helped with recovery. I was fed, *overfed* by my family. My dad and mom make sure I got the nutrients I needed. For the last six moments—months, I've been wrapped in love. When I got to the place I'm at now, I started feeling that I needed to push myself. That I need to push. So, here I am."

"So coming here on your own is your taking control."

She smiled. "Yes. I had to. My family knows I'm blessed to have my brain back in an amazing way. It still has more to go or maybe it's as far as it will go. But I'm here because I wanted to be here. I need to know that I can function on my own, even if I can't get all my words right. So, I'm finally writing a book, stitching my creative brain."

He smiled, and unable to help himself, he reached out and hugged her and didn't tell her she'd said stitching her creative mind instead of stretching. His heart exploded when she hugged him back.

Forcing his words to be steady, he said, "You've got this." Then he hugged her tighter, gently, then released her.

He had to release her. This attraction that had grabbed him wasn't in good timing. He couldn't put any kind of pressure on her, no matter how much he wanted to keep her in his arms.

They talked more while they ate. The doctors had told her it would take time to know just how much of her memory she'd lost, though they assured her that nothing would get worse. Her words dug deep.

"I'm as bad as I'm going to get and so I constantly remind myself to be grateful for the progress my inflamed brain has made. I won't let myself feel sorry for me so don't you either."

"I won't. I admire you. You, Lana Valentine, are a

fighter. So, you started writing a book?" It was time to change that subject. She needed to relax and get comfortable and there was more about her he was interested in.

She nodded. "I am. I loved reading about Mule Hol…low," she finished with a pause. "My brain has behaved in a miraculous way during recovery as I walk and dictate, even though it might not seem that is has. I'm dictating a romance about a cowboy and a recoverin—" She stopped talking and it wasn't like the other times when she'd faltered. Her face turned pink, she ripped her eyes away from his, and stared out at the river.

"What's wrong?" Jeb moved closer to her, startled by her shocked expression and needing to help.

"Nothing, I…I'm not ready to talk about my book." She waved a hand toward the water. "Can we stop talking about me and go toss some rocks in the river?"

"That's a great idea." He stood up and held a hand out to her. She slid her hand into his and stood. "Maybe you just need some relaxation and no worries. If you say something wrong, let it go. I'm not worried about it."

"Okay, I'm working at just that and so with you, I just won't worry." They smiled at each other and then walked down a cow path to the water's edge.

As they tossed rocks into the water, they talked about regular things. Like how pretty it was here on the ranch and about the water. She told him about life, helping her dad make famous spurs.

And she relaxed.

When she saw a buzzard flying above them, she said, "Do you have a lot of broadcast flying over?"

He looked up and laughed, "I see them all the time."

They laughed together hard and relief spread through him. And then they kept on talking.

CHAPTER EIGHT

By Tuesday, Lana had gone to the grocery store, picked up supplies, and finished unpacking. She was feeling happy about her move to Mule Hollow. Her time spent with Jeb had eased her mind some and she was thankful he'd been there for her. Just thankful. Now, she started work at Hailey Bell's real estate office tomorrow and felt better about it after spending time with Jeb. Hailey had wanted her to get settled in before she came into the office and Lana really appreciated that. She'd needed settling in more than she'd realized.

Earlier that morning she'd talked to her sister, who had assured her things were going good at home. Knowing that relieved a little stress and helped her settle in better. Lana had made the right choice. Before she had gotten sick, she'd been working with the family company but had wanted to step away and work on her writing but she hadn't done it. Theirs was a family business and she felt bad walking away.

But, knowing the writing process helped with recovery helped her know which direction she wanted to go with her life. Besides that, her sister loved creating the spurs and was fantastic at marketing them therefore, everything had worked out well.

Today was the day she was looking forward to. Lana had made an appointment for a haircut and so she headed down the sidewalk toward the bright pink two-story Heavenly Inspirations salon. She'd said she had no preference of a stylist because she'd heard both were wonderful. As it happened, Lacy was slipping her into her schedule while Izzy worked on coloring Esther Mae's hair. That meant the room would be filled with entertainment that had nothing to do with her mixed-up words. Sweet Esther Mae would take the show with ease.

Lana waved at Applegate and Stanley as she passed by the first window of the diner. They grinned at her and waved back. She was about to cross the road when she heard her name being called.

"Lana," Jeb called again from where he was standing outside of Pete's Feed and Seed a little further down the street.

Her pulse skipped as she smiled then walked his way. "Hey, are you picking up supplies?" she asked, completely thrilled to see him. She'd loved walking along the river with him and tossing rocks in the water. She'd been able to talk to him and not worry about whether her words were going to come out wrong. It had been so helpful. Every time he'd laughed at what she said wrong because it usually was funny, made her relax more and enjoy the twinkle in his amazing eyes.

"I am. I'm actually about to go make a fence repair on the backside of the property. If you'd like to go back out, I can wait until you can go."

Out again. He'd just asked her to go with him again, her brain rolled over it with joy. Joy that she wasn't completely comfortable feeling but what the heck. "I would love t! I really enjoyed it out by the river. I was wondering if you would mind if I come out there and walk along the water's edge two or three days a week and get some dictating and exercise all at the same time."

"Sure. Anything I can do to help you and your recovery I'll do." He smiled and her heart did a backflip.

"Thanks," she said, suddenly breathless. "So where do I meet you to repair the fence? My appointment will probably take about an hour if you have time to wait."

"I can wait. Meet me at the theater barn. We'll go to the land behind it."

"That sounds great. See you then."

"Okay, I'll be there." He took a step back, but his eyes were still on her and hers on him.

Hair, her brain screamed at her thankfully. "I've got a haircut." She turned and hurried across the street, tossing a glance each way to make sure she didn't get run over.

She made it to the salon, resisting the urge to look over her shoulder to see if he might still be standing there looking better than any man had ever looked.

What was wrong with her?

Before she could open the door, it swung open by a

grinning Esther Mae. The redhead's wide grin stretched from almost ear to ear. She had squares of foil cascading all across her head like a huge square sliver halo alternating with strips of red hair poking everywhere. "Come on in here. I want to hear about what's going on between you and our new singin' cowboy."

"I stink—I mean I…" She'd messed that up because she was all disoriented from her interaction with Jeb and now foil-clad Esther Mae; nothing right was coming out.

"That was cute. And you don't stink." Esther Mae laughed.

"I meant I *think* y'all are wrong."

"I don't stink so," Esther Mae said with a laugh. "I often get my words mixed up. So are you copying me to try and get our minds off the cowboy and you?"

"Esther Mae gets a lot of words mixed up," Norma Sue said, cutting into the conversation as she came out of the back room carrying a red mug that had the word coffee written on it in big white letters. "Actually, she isn't as bad now as she used to be. Y'all remember when she said she wanted a pair of Neutazlizers?"

"Yes!" Lacy exclaimed as she and everyone else, including Esther Mae, laughed. The woman's head of silver shook she laughed so hard. Then her gaze came back to Lana. "I meant *Naturalizers*." She lifted her foot up and showed her low-healed shoe. "These are so comfortable I wear them all the time. And now they have a bunch of wonderful styles to choose from."

"They do look comfortable, and…cute," Lana said, trying hard not to mess up again.

"Dear," Adela said, her voice soft. "You don't have to worry about saying things wrong. Applegate, Stanley, and my Sam told us you said a few things oddly and they were worried about you."

"They aren't worried about me," Esther Mae declared. "They know things just come out of my mouth all golfed up—goofed up sometimes." She hooted with laughter.

Lana laughed too, not sure if she'd meant to say golfed or was just playing with everyone, but the lady was funny.

"Seriously," Lacy said. "You look like it bothers you and we want you to know that you can relax around us instead of looking all worried when it comes out wrong."

Her gaze scanned the room and all the ladies, young and old, were smiling—or feeling sorry for her. "You are all nice and you don't have to feel sorry for me. I do get words wrong—thankfully my brain knows what it meant to say."

"We don't mind," Izzy said. "My sweet grams— they got words mixed up too but they were a *lot* older than all of you ladies."

"That's the truth," Esther Mae declared. "If I reach one hundred and seven like your grammy there's no telling what's coming out of my mouth."

Everyone chuckled and Lana relaxed at the encouragement.

Lacy patted the table—the *chair* for her to sit down in. She realized she even got the word mixed up in her thoughts that time. She sat down and placed her palms on her knees. "So, here is my story—" And she told them quickly what she'd been through. "But I'm doing great now. I get my words messed up—a lot. But I'm trying to fib—" She chuckled at her goof. "*Fix* it over time."

Everyone laughed again and she did too, and tears came into her eyes.

"Honey, don't cry," Norma Sue demanded. "It's okay. We've got your back now that we know what's going on."

Lacy bent over and gave her a hug. "Girl, you came to the right place. We'll support you all the way. You just talk and get to doing that dictating you were talking about that helped you. If God gave you that idea and it's working, then go for it. I want to read that book when it's done."

"I do too," the manicurist called out from where she sat at her manicure table. "I'm Sheri, the friend who rode into town in that topless pink Caddy with Lacy several years ago. You keep going and let that brain heal. As much as I didn't believe it on that first day we drove into town, well, Mule Hollow is the place to be for help in so many ways. You've come to the right place."

Lana couldn't help the tears that came then, tears of thankfulness. "Frank— Thank y'all," she managed as the tears rolled down her cheeks. Everyone huddled around her and wrapped her in a big supportive embrace.

"I think we should pray," Adela said.

"You've got that right," Norma Sue agreed.

Speechless, Lana nodded, her gaze touching on each of the women who looked at her with such caring and love. And so, Adela prayed.

She prayed that God would heal Lana in His way and time and give her peace. And she quoted a verse that touched Lana's heart, "For we walk by faith, not sight." At that, Lana looked up and met Adela's smiling eyes. The older lady added, "Or words. In You we trust, Amen."

The verse came from 2 Corinthians 5:7. Lana had read it just that morning and it had rang true for her. It was as if God was letting her know this was what she needed to do, He'd given it to Adela too.

She smiled. "Thank you. Yes, I'm trusting Him and walking by faith and grateful for where I am in my healing…right words or wrong words. I'm happy to be alive and grateful. God is giving me healing by His grace. There are far worse things going on with people in the world, so this…this is just a small thing." And she meant it. She was smiling inside and out as was everyone in the room.

God was so good.

"*Awwe*some," Lacy sang. "Now, let's have some fun. What do you want me to do with this beautiful, thick, wavy hair you've been blessed with?"

Lana grinned broadly. "Whatever you want. I'm feeling free and adventurous."

That got her squeals of delight from everyone, and Lacy went to work!

CHAPTER NINE

Jeb's heart was racing as he waited beside the big barn. He tapped his fingers on the side of the truck, knowing good and well his heart was going crazy because Lana was coming to ride beside him again.

He'd tried not to let what was going on inside his head spin out of control. Tried to tell himself that it was too soon to think about someone like he'd started thinking about the woman who tossed rocks in the river with him a few days ago.

The woman he was waiting on.

The woman who'd stepped out on her own despite what had happened to her. It inspired him—that was why his heart was acting funny, he tried to tell himself.

The sound of the Jeep had him standing straight up,

and he watched her speeding down the dirt road, dust rising behind her. Her hair was twirling in the wind, nothing holding it back. He laughed as she pulled up to him and came to an abrupt halt. The dust settled. Thank goodness the wind was blowing away from them or they'd have been smothered in it.

"Hey, sorry I'm late." She sprang from the Jeep.

"You're not late and…" he started, lost for words. She'd put on boots, jeans, and a light blue shirt. Her hair was settled around her face like cascading dark fluffy waves. "I like your hair."

"Oh, thanks," she said, raking it from her face. "I told Lacy to do it her way and she gave me a similar cut, but my curl has more freedom now." She laughed. "It can slap me in the face while I'm driving with no top on—no top on my *Jeep*. Thank goodness I remembered to put a top on." She laughed, really laughed.

He loved it and laughed too and almost reached for her, but got hold of himself before he did that. The last thing she needed right now was a cowboy messing up her recovery and taking away her sparkle.

But maybe she could handle him as a friend.

"I like your blouse," he said, and they both laughed harder. She placed her hand on his arm ,which sent an electric bolt of massive voltage spiking through him. "You ready to go watch me fix a fence?"

She pulled her hand away. "I want to try to help you, I'm from a ranch too. But I never really helped with fence building so I might need my hero in my book fixing a fence. If so, I'll need to know how to do it."

"Okay, sounds good. Anything I can do to help give you something for your book I'll do. Or I'll connect you with the cowboy who can."

"Thank you. I'm ready.

"Hop in and we'll head out."

She strode to passenger side of the truck and slid in as he got behind the steering wheel. "I'm assuming since you ride without that top on your Jeep you're okay with the windows being down," he teased.

"How did you know?" She grinned and put her arm out the window like she was ready to hug the sky. "I love the feel of the wind. It lets me know I'm alive."

She was definitely alive. Every cell in his body and heart knew it.

* * *

They drove through the ranch and the beautiful countryside. Cattle grazed in many of the pastures. Lana was so glad she'd seen him that morning and he'd asked her to do this. And she'd relaxed some after being around the ladies at Heavenly Inspirations. So, now she focused on the scenery, tried to anyway, but it was hard not to let her gaze go back to Jeb. He looked like a cowboy hero, and her mind kept going to the character in her book, rewriting his description—

Don't do that. Right, if this book were to ever get published, then she didn't want anyone knowing…what? *That you are infatuated with Jeb*…she yanked her thoughts from going where she wasn't ready to go.

"What's that?" she asked, grateful something odd had grabbed her attention. They were in a lower area of pastures and the trees had mesh wire five feet up their trunks.

He slowed down so she could see it better. "That's a galvanized weld mesh tree wrap. It's to keep the beavers I was telling you about from chewing down the trees, building dams, blocking the river, and making this area into a lake."

"Wow, I've lived in Texas my whole life and that's the first time I've actually seen a tree wrapped like that. My dad's ranch never had them."

"They're usually in places like this, off the main roads where they aren't disturbed. These were built several years ago, maybe five or six, when Sugar Rae and Ross were getting to know each other."

"Right, you said the beavers were resolved—involved."

He grinned. "Resolved actually works. Yes, beavers helped them realize they were falling in love. One tried to attack Sugar Rae's toes, stole her sandal actually. She loves to tell the story of how Ross swept her into his arms and was her hero."

Lana loved it. "How wonderful. And funny. I'd tell that story too. And it happened here."

It was happening here again, not that she was getting attacked by a beaver, but Jeb was definitely falling in love. "Yep, here." He pressed the gas, and soon they were across the bridge that got them to the far side of the ranch where the damaged fence was waiting.

Falling in love. The thought echoed in his brain. He needed to work. Needed something to concentrate on and take his mind off the woman riding in his truck. The woman he'd only known for a very short few days. He pulled to a halt parallel to the fence that needed to be fixed. "And here we go. Hop out and I'll show you how it's done."

"Awesome. This will be fun."

He got out, strode to the back of the truck, and let the tailgate down. Then he pulled the needed supplies to the edge. "Wear these." He handed her a pair of leather gloves. "I'll let you help me stretch out a section of the wire fence then you can watch. It's not a big job, but you don't need to overdo it." He refused to be responsible for her doing too much.

"Thanks. In all honesty, my body tells me what I can do and then it repels—I mean…" She laughed at the word that had come out her mouth. "*Forces* me into resting—whether I want to or not."

He smiled gently. "God has a way of keeping

overachievers in line." Jeb had a feeling that was exactly what she was.

She pulled the gloves on. "Precisely. Now, show me what to do."

"Okay, we'll get busy but tell me when I need to repel you." That made her laugh. And her laugh made him laugh.

"You're funny."

"Can't help it, I like your laugh." He meant it.

"I'm glad you invited me out today."

They stared at each other and then, before he messed up their friendship with the kiss he so wanted to give her, he picked up the roll of barbed wire and moved to the fence. She followed him. "I'll unload the tools; you relax before I put you to work."

"Okay, boss." She smiled.

He grinned, then headed back to the truck to grab the post-hole digger.

"Oh," she called out. "This is a gully—"

Jeb spun at her words, heart thundering. She'd left the side of the downed fence and crossed the short space to the edge of the gully—ravine actually where it dropped off into the downhill rough rolling slope and then had a not to nice drop into a muddy curve of the river bed.

"Get back!" he shouted as she looked over her shoulder at him. At that moment, just as he feared, what looked like firm ground gave way beneath Lana's feet taking her with it.

"*No*," he yelled, rushing forward, his hand outstretched but she was already crashing down toward the drop.

* * *

Lana had been feeling so alive, odd words or not. But now, with barely time to scream, she was rolling down the weed-covered embankment. At the edge she flew into the air and landed flat on her back in the mud.

"Thank you, Lord," she managed as she caught her breath looking up just in time to see Jeb plunge over the drop-off and come flying down into the mud beside her.

He grunted as he, instead of landing on his back like she did, landed on his belly, his face in the mud.

She pushed up on her elbows, ignoring the pain, knowing if the mud hadn't been there, it would have been much worse. "Jeb," she said, worried because he hadn't moved. "Jeb." She forced herself to sit up, planning to roll him out of the mud. She got to her knees, grabbed his right shoulder and, with every ounce of strength she had, rolled him over. His muddy eyes were closed.

Then they flew open, and he instantly sat up. "What happened?"

"I—," Lana started to say, but before she got anything else out he reached for her.

"Are you alright?" he asked, pulling her into his muddy lap, his hands running along her arms. He cupped her face with his mud-covered hands and looked at her with his golden eyes that were surrounded by black mud.

She smiled. Then laughed. And before she could stop herself, she leaned into him and let her lips touch his muddy lips. Thankfully the taste of the mud brought her to her senses, and she pulled back. "Sorry."

Jeb grinned with his slightly less muddy lips.

"Don't be. I would say that would mean that you are okay and in your right mind. But then again, kissing muddy me might mean you're all messed up."

She laughed hard at those funny words. "I'm definitely all messed up," she sang, and then placed her muddy hand against his cheek. "And so are you."

He wrapped his arms around her and pulled her to lean against him. "Are you hurt?" Concern rang in his voice, and it touched her deeply as did being held in his arms.

She'd had so many people who loved her during her messed-up time, and she loved them dearly, but something about this moment and this man struck a deep chord in her soul and pulled her in. "I'm sorry you misstopped—stepped and followed me down this gully."

"I didn't misstep, I freely jumped trying to get to you."

They stared at each other. Then mud and all, he kissed her again, a deep kiss that reached inside of her and pulled emotions she'd never felt before from her. She hugged him tight as the kiss ended and he rested his forehead against her shoulder.

Lana's heart pounded harder than it had during the fall and she wanted to cuddle closer if that were possible.

"Come on," he said, his voice gruff with emotion. He shifted her from his lap, then he stood up, still holding her hand as he helped her stand. "We need to ease our way back up this slope and back to sanity."

"Sanity?" she asked, standing still.

"Yes." He looked troubled. "I'm sorry I must have been out of my mind bringing you out here. I'm sorry I didn't warn you about that drop-off. Sorry, I've put you at risk."

That was it. He felt guilty. "I'm fine."

"Thank the good Lord and not me." His frustration and anger at himself was now very clear. He tugged her hand and started up the embankment in a slow progression and she followed. He said nothing as they went, his hand firm on hers, his booted feet sure-footed with each step he took, leading the way back to the top of the ridge and straight to the passenger side of the truck.

"Let's get cleaned up and get you back to your apartment so you can rest."

She was tired but she didn't want to be, she wanted to be back in his arms. He reached into the back of the truck and pulled out several rags, handing her two. "I keep these in here for cleaning up my hands after working out in the boonies."

He wiped his face and his hands. She wanted to tell him she wasn't tired, but her body had given out. And she wasn't at all sure what else to say. The man was clearly shaken up.

"Thanks," she said as she wiped her face and hands. Then he opened the passenger door and helped her as she climbed into the seat. There was no use saying she was sorry for getting his truck dirty because he was going to do the same. Besides, she suddenly had no words to say.

If she spoke, the words she wanted to say might not come out sounding right…but she had a feeling if she accidently said she loved him, she would mean it.

Loved him.

The roll down the hill had shaken her up too. She

kept her mouth firmly shut because right now, she couldn't risk making another mistake. Especially of that magnitude.

What had happened to her brain had been none of her doing. It had slammed into her out of nowhere. It was a miracle how she had overcome the illness and recovered as she had. She knew to whom to give the glory and credit for the healing.

But, where this man who was driving her to her Jeep was concerned…if she messed up when her mind wasn't totally where it needed to be, she could only blame herself. So she kept her lips tight.

They reached her Jeep and he parked. "Are you sure you can drive? I can drive you back to town and get you to your room—"

"No, I'm fine. We may both hurt tomorrow but neither of us hit our heads on anything. My words are even right."

"Right. Okay, I'll check on you."

"No. I'm fine. Go fix your fence and don't worry about me." She got out of the truck, ignoring the aches and glad there weren't many. "I start work tomorrow so

I should rest up anyway."

"Yes, I should have thought of that earlier."

"No," she said, almost in a growl. "*I* should have thought of it. I'm the one living in this body." And with that she climbed into her Jeep and turned the key. The engine blasted to life like the anger suddenly blasting through her.

This was one of the reasons she'd come here on her own. *She* wanted to be responsible for her life. She needed to be responsible and know that she could make it on her own. And falling in love with all this before her was a bad, bad thing.

He stared at her, taken aback by her anger. Thankfully he just nodded and lifted his hand in goodbye. Feeling a little guilty, she lifted hers and then grabbed the dirty pink steering wheel with a vice grip. Then she pressed the gas pedal and drove the Jeep in a wide circle then headed back toward town.

If only getting back to normal was as easy as driving her Jeep.

CHAPTER TEN

This was crazy. She slapped the steering wheel in frustration. She was tired of being tired. *Tired* of not saying words right. Tired of not knowing—*things*. All sorts of things. Things she once took for granted.

She gripped the steering wheel even harder with semi-muddy hands and glared at the road before her. She'd been the one who'd walked to the edge of that *ravine*—there she'd called it the right word at least. She'd been the one who hadn't been careful enough to look to see if the edge was safe.

And that was what worried her.

Was that something she would always have to worry about? The thinking but not *really* thinking correctly? Was she always going to have to worry about her sanity, her decision-making being off?

Her phone rang from the cup holder—the clean phone she'd forgotten to put in her pocket, thank goodness.

She picked it up, glanced down at the screen and saw it was her dad. Instantly she pulled over onto the side of the road, put the Jeep in park, and answered.

"Dad, hello," she gushed, knowing she sounded more stressed out than he needed to hear.

"Are you alright?" he asked, the worry in his voice telling her that she indeed sounded stressed out. She was too tired to try to cover up how upset she was.

"I'm, well Dad, I'm mad. But I'm okay, sorry. Just a little fed up with my memory…what is it, loss or craziness?" she blurted the words out with the frustration and anger welling inside of her.

"Calm down," he said gently. "Are you sitting down?"

"Yes, I—" She stopped talking, at least having the sense not to tell him she'd been driving while having an angry breakdown. "I'm sitting down." There, that wasn't a lie.

"Good. I've been wondering and a little worried about when you were going to get irritated about all of this. Getting angry is good. Normal. You needed to let it go. You handled this brain infection like a champ, you know," he said, his voice still gentle and calming.

"So, you tell me," she replied. Lana was immensely thankful for him.

"Lana, you were so weak and out of it when they injected the meds in you, but you started responding quickly. You needed your bloodwork constantly and you know how hard it is to get blood out of your veins, even when you were a kid. But they had to do a lot of testing on you. It's always taken by someone who really knew what they were doing to get blood out of your runaway veins. But they got the blood despite your ornery veins."

She smiled. "I know. It's like even my veins don't like being bullied."

"True. They take after their owner. Anyway, I want to tell you this again in case you forgot about me telling you before. I know you don't remember anything that went on in that hospital during those first three weeks.

You were so weak and had to relearn a lot, including walking and getting words out, but you worked at it. But the ornery veins were where you shined. Those professional nurses had to stick you so many times trying to get blood but your rolling veins sidestepped them over and over. But, you sat there in that bed so sweetly and told them each time it was okay." Her dad's voice wobbled with emotion. "Even in pain you were sweet."

"I'm so glad I was nice," she said.

He laughed gently. "You were. So many things were new to you, even holding a fork. You could hardly hold a fork, but one day when one of the sweet maids came in, you pointed to a piece of paper and asked me for it. With a pencil you wrote the cleaning lady a note."

Her heart clenched at hearing all this again. She'd been through this and so had her dad, right there by her side, never leaving. It affected him now as it had then.

"That note looked like a four-year-old wrote it, but it meant so much to me and the cleaning lady. You told her in crooked words what a good job she was doing. It told us how sweet you were…and are."

She didn't feel sweet right now, as the anger surged in her again. "I'm so glad I was. I'm so glad you were there with me and are still with me right now. But I'm tired of this, Dad."

"Do you need me to come get you?"

"No. I'm just frustrated." She rubbed her temple again.

"Relax. Remember you surprised me when you woke up in all that pain that night before we were to come home. That hard pain woke your brain up. But, until that moment you fooled us all." He chuckled, and she loved hearing that chuckle. "Thank goodness that happened and I didn't bring you home with lungs full of blood clots. But before I knew you weren't consciously with me, you passed your physical test of walking down the hall and walking up a flight of stairs. That was a great feeling because I had to catch you several times during recovery when your legs gave way. You don't remember but one time you were at the sink after accomplishing brushing your teeth on your own—you told me you could do it—and then I saw you wobble and rushed to catch you. You went limp as could be.

Fortunately, I knew the lounge chair was behind me and we fell into it. The nurses came running because the monitors all went off and there we lay, slumped in the chair all tangled up. And those wonderful nurses helped get you off of me and into bed. I thank God every day I was there by your side to keep you from falling and hurting yourself more."

Tears ran down her cheeks and her anger subsided as gratefulness took over. She couldn't speak, instead she closed her eyes and thanked God for all He'd done for her.

"Darlin', you've come a long, a *long* way and you don't need to forget that."

She took a deep breath and opened her eyes. "You're right," she whispered. "Thanks, Dad, I needed a reminder."

"And I just needed to hear your voice and the good Lord had me call at the right time."

She smiled. "His timing is always right—"

"Even if we don't like it," her father finished with her.

It was true. She knew that. She sighed. "Thank you

for the reminder of how far I've come."

"You're welcome. Now, do you mind telling me what set this off or have you been feeling like this since you drove out of my driveway?"

"I love you dearly, but I need the space. It's been not even a week since I drove away. And it's acute—actually been a great week. Today was just a hard moment."

"I was praying it was a good week for you. A new beginning."

She smiled and rubbed her temple. "I know you've been praying and thank you. I just…" She laughed. "I just fell down a muddy ridge. A very nice cowboy dove down after me trying to save me—don't get alarmed, I'm not hurt and he isn't either. We're just really muddy and I…"

"You what?" her dad asked. "You sure you're okay, and is this a good guy?"

"Yes, to both. I just…well, I'm really attracted to him and he knows what I've been through and wants to help me. But, Dad, I want to make this on my own for now. I'm afraid to add the strain of thinking,

I'm…sorry, I've said a lot and haven't said anything wrong as far as I know. But I need to rest. I'll talk about this later."

"Alright, just promise me you'll rest and call me if you need me. I'm giving you space but I'm here. And you will make it. You already have come an amazing long way."

"Thanks for the much needed reminder. I love you."

"And I love you. Now, go rest and keep on fighting. Your brain is good, it just needs rest and a good workout. Have you been writing, dictating, and reading?"

She smiled. "Yes, and tomorrow I work at the real estate company so answering phones hopefully will help too. I think that surely I can direct calls."

"You can. Go for it."

They said goodbye again and she checked the quiet road before pulling out and heading home. She had a new day waiting for her tomorrow and every day she was granted was one more than she might have had.

And that was something she need not ever forget.

Every day she lived was a gift. Maybe if she wrote something good, something from her heart, she could touch someone. Maybe it would help them overcome something they were going through.

She refocused on that thought. God had given her a new shot at touching someone and she was going to use a love story to do just that.

She just had to remember that the book was her new goal.

Personally, falling in love was not on her goal list. Maybe it would be one day when she could be sure her heart and brain were communicating coherently. And that wasn't completely where she was yet.

* * *

Esther Mae, Norma Sue, and Adela sat in a booth near the window drinking coffee at Sam's. After having hung out in the hair salon far longer than Lacy, Izzy or Sheri probably wanted they had come to Sam's for lunch. And now Sam kept coming by to make sure his sweet Adela had everything she needed.

Esther Mae sighed as he walked off. "You made him a happy man when you finally married him six years ago." So much had happened in their little town since the three of them had become the Posse. They had prayed hard, waiting for women to answer their ads and come to town to meet their future husbands. "I sure love our lives," she said with meaning.

"I do too," Norma Sue agreed.

"And you know I agree too." Adela smiled and her blue eyes twinkled. "You two have really gotten into trouble and made me increase my prayers."

Esther Mae tapped her hair and grinned. "Your prayers have helped work wonders. I think God really listens to you."

"Prayers are powerful, and you know it."

Esther grinned. "Yes, I just have to tease you. So, are we going to talk about what we can do to help get Jeb and Lana—" As she spoke, she looked out the window just as a mud-covered Lana drove by in her Jeep. She'd looked great two hours ago when she'd left the hair salon. "Did y'all see Lana? She's covered in what looks like mud."

"What?" Norma Sue exclaimed, looking out the window.

Adela stood up instantly, obviously having seen what Esther Mae saw. "Yes. Come on. We need to check on her." She headed toward the door and Esther Mae and Norma Sue followed her.

"What's wrong?" Sam asked.

"They saw Lana," App barked. "She looks like she jumped in a mud hole." He stood up and Stanley did too.

Esther Mae thought they were all going to march down the sidewalk to see what happened, but Adela turned toward the men.

"Sam, Applegate, and Stanley—I believe we ladies need to take care of this. But your concern is touching. We've got this."

"Okay," App growled. "But if that sweet girl—woman…needs us, you let us know."

Esther Mae grinned. "You know we will. She's made buddies out of you three."

They nodded and then backed off as Sam opened the door for them. The women walked quickly down the sidewalk. They got to the end of the walk just as Lana got out of the Jeep. She was definitely covered in drying mud.

"What happened?" Norma Sue demanded, then added, "honey, I've worked a lot of cattle on a muddy day, but you look like you took a dive off the end of a slide and landed in a huge mud hole."

Lana sighed. "That is exactly what I did. It was a wild ride and thankfully a soft landing. I spat—splattered…mud all over the place. The sky is beautiful when you're lying in a mud hole looking up at it."

Her words were light and teasing.

"Did you really?" Esther Mae asked, dumbfounded by how covered in mud she was and how good-natured she was about it.

"I did," Lana said, looking at them all.

Adela smiled and said gently, "You take things well. But you look like a shower and some rest is what you need. Did you have lunch?"

Lana shook her muddied head. "No, I didn't have lunch, but I have plenty of food in the apartment."

"Then come on," Adela said. "We'll get you upstairs and while you take that shower, we will get you fixed up with lunch."

"Sure will," Esther Mae said, unable to not be

curious. "And if you want to tell us what happened, we'll be glad to listen."

"I really—" Lana started to say.

Norma Sue stepped up to her. "Honey, you look slap worn out, you have mud caked all over you, and there is no way I'm letting you go up that set of steps without me following you to pad you if you were to fall down."

Lana tilted her dried mud hair to the side. "You really would do that for me? And y'all are right, I'm worn out. So…"

"So, I'll lead the way," Adela said calmly. "And you follow me."

"And we'll follow you," Esther Mae agreed, loving Lana, who calmly did as Adela said.

Norma Sue went after Lana and Esther Mae followed, holding onto the railing tight just in case. If sweet Lana did stumble, and she very likely could, and Norma did not stand her ground, then Esther Mae was going to have to slow them down.

Halfway up the stairs, Esther Mae sent up a prayer. Adela got the door opened and then with a few steps more, they each entered the safety of the apartment.

"I'll be back," Lana said, then turned and looked at them. "Thanks. One day I'll be back to normal." She headed into her bedroom then paused at the doorway and looked back at them. "Actually, I might not ever be back completely the way I was before. But I'm going to try and if not, I'm going to be okay with it. I'm blessed to be able to—" She stopped talking. "Be here."

And then she closed the door and the three women all looked at each other.

Norma Sue whispered, "What in the world happened? Do you think she was out dictating like she said she wanted to do and fell in the mud?"

"Maybe," Esther Mae said. "But we have to stay around and make sure she's okay in case she hit her head."

"She was driving straight," Adela said. "So, I think she's okay, but we need to make sure. We'll feed her and ask a few questions."

Norma Sue had just gotten some tomato soup heated up, Adela had made a ham sandwich, and Esther Mae had poured some sweet tea, when the bedroom door opened and a clean Lana walked out.

"You look better," Esther Mae said, relieved.

"I am. But y'all were right, I'm hungry."

"Come on over here." Adela placed the soup and sandwich plate on the table and Norma Sue pulled the chair out for her.

Esther Mae put the iced tea on the table then sat in the chair across from her. "What happened to you?"

Lana took a sip of her tea. "I made progress." And then she told them what happened.

She really had rolled down a hill and landed in the mud. And that handsome Jeb had landed beside her.

She smiled at them. "And yes, just like you ladies are thinking, he's awesome and I kissed him there in the mud. But just so you know…I can rarely—*barely* get my words straight. My mind is making autumn progress. *Awesome* progress. And that's what I have to focus on. You would never believe how far I've come since I got sick. My dad reminded me when he called at exactly the right time on my way home. I have to focus on what God's put in my muddled head and write my book, which is exercise for my brain. I have to give it my focus and that means that me and Jeb will just be friends."

CHAPTER ELEVEN

"So, how's it going over there?" Hailey Bell asked as she came in the door after having shown a property to a couple that morning.

"It's going well. You've had a few calls. One of them was a lady who has been visiting a lot and is thinking about buying some property around here."

"Great. Did you set up a date?"

"Yes, next week. Is that okay?"

"You bet. So, how is everything else going? You've got everything ready at your apartment, and I heard that you went to the show and loved it. And then I heard— *yes,* I hear a lot." Hailey paused when she saw Lana's eyes widen—"That you had a little mud day yesterday."

Hailey was wonderful and knew how to sell real

estate. And tell her story—what a story it was. She'd been a success in California real estate but had come back to Mule Hollow after she'd run away to find herself—as she'd put it. Before she'd run away to California, Hailey had fallen in love with Will Sutton but had gotten cold feet after realizing she had to find herself and she'd fled to California.

"What?" Hailey asked.

"I was just thinking about you and your husband. You were engaged two or three times before you got married, but you made it back to him."

Hailey grinned. "It's amazing, but yes. I ran away the first time because I'd let everyone take care of me and protect me. Unknowingly, my sweet first love, Will, was among them. I ran away to California to prove to myself that I wasn't a world-class mess-up. I made it through real estate classes. But I still made wrong moves. I could sell real estate really well. But, marrying? Goodness I ran away from three men."

Lana sat down. "But you and Will found each other again."

Hailey smiled. "Life has a way of working out.

Depending on the plan. God's plan. His timing. Timing is what matters and hearts that know where they belong. Me and Will found our way back to each other after all that I did wrong."

"I'm glad," Lana said, knowing she was also trying to find her way.

"But Will had done some things wrong too, so we both had things we had to work out. And in God's timing we got it right and are so happy now. I'll never forget on my way into town again when I was worn out, upset, and still wearing my wedding dress from the last wedding I'd run away from…who was the first person I saw when I got stopped in the middle of the road because the cows were out? Will. God works in mysterious ways."

Lana liked that Hailey and Will had managed to find each other again and worked their love for each other out. They now had two small children, which was why she only worked three days a week.

"How about you? Are you here looking for love and ready to be targeted by the Posse? I guess you know you and Jeb have a big spot on their vision board."

Vision board. "I never thought about that." Maybe she needed a vision board for her life. And as far as being targeted by the Posse? She didn't think she could do that.

Her brain went to how she'd left Jeb yesterday. "No, he's a great guy. But right now, as you probably heard. I'm overcoming viral encephalitis, and it takes some concentration. And some work. My brain has enough to recover by exercising it in many ways. Working here is good. I'm exercising it by answering phones and writing things down. To be honest, I'm stumbling over a few words. I made a mistake on the last call and the nice lady just laughed and said she makes more mistakes than me calling her the wrong name." She hesitated.

"It's okay," Hailey said.

"Thanks, names are my worst part. You'll notice I don't call people by their names often because what my mind is thinking and what comes out of my mouth doesn't always match. Then add the silly words that come out at the end of a sentence—oh, believe me, I can be *very* entertaining. And annoying. So if I ever say anything that's not right, please correct me. Or if you think this will harm your business, I can step away." There she'd said it. She should have warned Hailey before she took the job.

"I love that you're pushing yourself. And this is the perfect job for you. Anything else that can help your brain wake up?"

"Yes, right after I got home from the hospital, I started dictating. That's helping my mind think more and communicate with my fingers because I listen to the words and type them. I haven't had a chance to do that since I got here. I was thinking I'd go walk and dictate by that field down the street y'all use for festivals after I get off work today."

"That all is amazing."

"Yes, it has been. The doctors said it's good for me and I love it. I've always dreamed about being a writer, and this illness got me focused on what I really want. So here I am starting over on my own and determined to succeed no matter how long it takes."

Hailey Bell's expression softened. "We have a lot of roads out at our place if you want to dictate and explore. New sights to see might help."

She thought about where she really wanted to go dictate—by Jeb's river. But she wasn't going out there now. She'd seen him enough in her first week here and she needed space. Her crazy brain was getting more confused. She'd come here to be on her own and not rely on her family, and she'd funneled it all up…*fumbled* it up getting stuck on Jeb.

And then she'd kissed him. She'd thought about that over and over—

"*Hello*," Hailey said in a singsong voice.

Lana gave a soft laugh. "And I do that. My brain gets sidetracked sometimes and that is where the writing helps. It's good if I can focus on something and get it out in dictation instead sitting in a chair with my fingers on a keyboard trying to get my brain to work. There's something about my feet doing the walking that makes my brain do the talking."

Hailey Bell smiled with happiness. "That is so wonderful."

Lana nodded. "It is. And it works."

"I love it and want to read your book when it's

done."

Her heart quickened at those words. "All I can say is I hope it's readable. I'll have to hire an editor who can make sure my words are right. And that I didn't miss any. But right now what matters is opening up my heart and mind and figuring things out each step of the way."

Hailey stood up and crossed the room to her, leaned in, and gave her a hug. "Believe me I understand, and I'm glad you are here. You know how to fix your words and recognize when you've said something wrong. I'm excited that you're here and that working for me can help you."

"Learning all the love stories here inspires me. I love reading all the tales Molly writes. Yesterday, I opened up to the ladies of the Posse about all of this too. I tried to hide it and I'm sorry I didn't tell you before you hired me. I just knew what I needed and wanted to come to Mule Hollow. This job was open so I applied."

Lana walked over to the window and Hailey did too.

"We all have a story," Hailey said. "Something we have to overcome. Believe me I know." She laughed.

"I'm going to get my story straight one way or the other. I'll get it right over time or I'll learn to live with it. So many people learn to live with far, far more problems than I'm having now."

"So true."

"I think I have my mind and heart right about that. I want to touch people—" *with my story*. She didn't say those words out loud, but it was in the back of her mind. Could she give one of her characters her problem? No, she wasn't ready to tackle that yet. She had to keep it simple right now, writing her first romance novel and it should not copy real life.

"If I do something and not know I did it wrong, please don't feel sorry for me. Let me know and I'll correct it. It's all good. So please, boss lady, let me know if I've messed up and I'll learn from it."

Hailey smiled, walked over to the open sign and changed it to closed. "You are going to do great. Now it's time for you to go do your dictating and for me to go see my hubby. He's making a new iron gate for someone. He loves doing that and is so amazingly good at it. So, let's say it's been a great day and head out."

"If you're sure, then I'm all in." And she was. Even though Lana was wearing a dress and sandals, she walked over to her Jeep, reached into the seat, and picked up her tiny tape recorder. Then, she headed across the street. It was time to dictate and take her story to another level. Her brain too.

She walked to the field and looked down the long grassland. This was where the town held fairs and gatherings. She hoped they had one soon. She couldn't wait. At the back of the field was a bunch of mesquite trees. Their curved trunks bent at sitting level would make great benches if she got tired and needed to sit down.

This was going to be good. She clicked the record button on her small recorder and started walking and talking and words flowed. She smiled as words came out. She loved it. Her hero and heroine were going to have a great happy ending when she got to that part. That was the key ingredient for the book she was writing…and for her. She was going to regain as much of her mind as possible and this walking, talking, and then typing was the way to do it.

Plus, she loved the feel of the wind on her skin and the sun shining down on her. Peace engulfed her and she knew she was where she was supposed to be and doing what she needed, wanted to do.

Her life was crazy but it seemed perfect in that moment.

CHAPTER TWELVE

Jeb had come to town the back way and parked behind Pete's. He needed to pick up the supplies for Ross. Now, here he stood at the front of the store, and instead of looking for what he needed he was looking out the front window. He saw Lana as she crossed the road, walked down the sidewalk, and into the open field where the town held festivals.

It looked like she was dictating and obviously wasn't going to come do it at his place by the river. The pasture she was walking in was good because it was close to town. It also had mesquite trees. Mesquite trees were great benches for conversations and great for cowboys to get out of the sun and rest. So they'd work for Lana if she got tired or just needed to sit down and rest. His heart hurt for what had happened at his place.

There, across the street, there were no slippery slopes for her to tumble down—he still hadn't forgiven himself for not warning her about the loose ground.

That field was probably a better place for her to be rather than alone out by the river on his place. He'd messed up by not warning her about the ravine. Thank goodness there was no ravine across the street.

He had a feeling she wasn't coming near him again for a while. He understood too. His throat clogged thinking about it. She'd kissed him. Thrown her arms around him and held him tight. He still felt her arms around him. It meant so much to him but then reality came into focus as she'd been holding him. He saw it in her eyes; she knew she needed this time for herself. And thank goodness the good Lord had slapped him on the head and told him to let her go.

So, here he stood, staying back, trying to give her freedom because this was her story, not his. He'd stepped back, as hard as it was to do when he knew with all of his heart he wanted her. But he understood. Where she was…he'd come to Mule Hollow to live his own story and not the story of his family on the stage.

He hadn't planned on Lana joining the plot, but he knew if he loved her—and he did—he would let her go. And so, he turned and walked through the back door, through the storage room, and to the deck where the truck was waiting.

Pete was standing on the deck watching Jeb's truck and trailer being loaded. "It's about ready."

"Thanks, Pete. It looks great, as always. You are a man who knows how to work your business."

Pete grinned. The heavyset man had a way about him. He didn't interrupt anyone, but he listened and was observant. Now he was just looking at Jeb.

"What?" Jeb asked.

"You seem a little different than when you first came to town. You seemed excited and ready to learn about this new life. You seem distant and pulled away now. Did something happen?"

"Yes, something happened. Sometimes you just have to adjust and that's what I'm doing. Do you know what I mean?"

"Sure, I had to adjust my desire to leave Mule

Hollow a long time ago. I wanted to grow up and leave but my life was here supporting all these ranchers. We may have a small town but the huge ranches need a lot of feed and seed and other things. And of course, I have to supply App and Stanley with their sunflower seeds so they can fill up their spittoon while they play checkers at Sam's and listen to everyone's business." He grinned. "So, I'm a man of all trades here in my store. And I like it. I'm glad I stayed. What's going on in that mind of yours?"

Jeb didn't say anything.

Pete cocked his head to the side. "I came in the door and saw you standing by the window watching down the street. You were deep in thought, so I didn't interrupt you. Instead, I eased on back out here. I wanted to let you contemplate whatever it was you were thinking about."

Jeb let out a dull laugh. "Yeah, I was watching. Watching a life I hadn't planned on and want, but I need to let go."

Pete crossed his arms and cocked his head to the other side studying Jeb. "God's timing. I see it a lot. I have a feeling I know who you're thinking about. App and Stanley came in for their sunflower seeds yesterday and said you might have a thing for our new resident."

He should have known. "Those two are sneaky old dudes."

"Yes, they are. And just so you know, they have their eyes on you and that sweet gal you're watching. But it's not their timing or the matchmakers' timing. It's you and Lana that matter. And, if it's meant to be it will happen when it happens. Me, I'll just enjoy listening to find out what happens in the story. And just so you know, you're the star of the story."

As he drove home Jeb thought about that. Was he part of a love story? Yes. Was it being written like he had thought it would be? So far nothing about it matched what he'd come here for. He didn't care. He just hoped that he got the ending he wanted. And right now he wasn't sure that was going to happen.

* * *

Lana had made progress. It was the end of her fourth

week in Mule Hollow and her second week of regularly coming out to the mesquite trees and dictating. She liked being out early in the morning watching the sunrise. It felt like she was way out in the boonies alone, but Mule Hollow was just a few yards away.

Her love story was coming along great. The one she was writing, not the one that teased at the back of her recovering brain. The one she'd let go of and obviously Jeb had too.

She'd been thankful the matchmakers had stepped back and were concentrating on her making mental health progress. The day they'd made sure she got to her apartment then got some rest had shown them how much she needed time.

Recovery could look easy, but it wasn't. The walking and the dictating were good for her brain, but she couldn't do as much as she wanted even though it had been seven months since she'd been released from the hospital. Seven months and her energy still gave out and her words still got fuddled up. The good thing about walking and dictating near her apartment meant she could just go up her stairs, sit in her blue chair beside the window, and rest.

She could sleep, type, or get distracted by looking out of the window and watch the folks of Mule Hollow drive in and out of the sweet town. It was the perfect place for her because it helped to get her brain thinking and creating stories about the people she didn't know.

She watched ladies going into the salon. Esther Mae, Norma Sue, and Adela went in often. They couldn't have possibly gotten their hair or nails done that often so they were probably just going to visit. If they weren't there, they were often at Sam's having coffee, sometimes at an outside porch. Even App and Stanley sat at a table and looked up at her on occasion. She waved at them a couple of times and other times pretended to be working on her computer. Yes, it was a fib, but she didn't want to move her chair but also didn't want to feel like she was a doll in a window.

That was one of the reasons she'd started coming out early in the morning to the mesquite trees and doing her dictating or just sitting and watching the sun come up while she prayed.

The town was still quiet at this time in the morning

when the sun was coming up. She loved this time of day. It was a new beginning, just like she was giving herself.

Lana was determined that if the words didn't come out like she wanted or needed them to, then she would adjust. She had to tell herself that less and less now as she was adjusting to hearing her crazy lips speak their own language sometimes. But she just reminded herself that she was adjusting and she kept on dictating and creating her book.

The story wasn't about her but there were troubles. She hoped her book would impact someone. The main character was overcoming a breakup and finding new love. Lana had started the storyline one way, then changed it, realizing that writing a book wasn't easy. She smiled. It wasn't easy but it made her happy. And it exercised her brain.

Just the backing up, rethinking situations, and coming up with different things to try worked her brain in fun and creative ways.

Now, as she sat there on the drooping tree trunk, she raked a hand through her wavy hair and thanked the Lord. Her words were getting better and she was determined to adapt. In the office if she messed something up, she and the customer or Hailey laughed about it and moved on. She had come to realize that messing up a word wasn't important; it was the way she reacted that was important. She'd decided that if she was supposed to give someone a laugh, then that was what she would gladly do. Maybe that was odd or she was odd but she was just fine with that.

She was adjusting, adapting, making the best of it. The one thing she was sure of was she was going to make it.

She stood up and walked toward town and headed toward Sam's. All the ladies were meeting because a rodeo was coming to town and they were going to run the concession stand. All the donations were going to No Place Like Home, a local women's shelter for abused women.

The ladies had asked Lana if she wanted to bake something for the concession stand and she'd laughed. She was a terrible cook and knew it, but she told them she could help take the money.

She could count money. She could count words

she'd written and the days of the year. She might have lost words but she could still do math.

She walked into the diner and the jukebox was playing, *"Goodness Gracious Great Balls of Fire"* loud and clear. Lana laughed because everyone was watching Esther Mae standing by the juke box swaying as she sang along.

"Fun," she said, then looked at Norma Sue.

Norma Sue was sitting at the table with a frown on her face. Applegate and Stanley were frowning too. Then Sam walked by and rolled his eyes.

"Is that not a good song?" she asked, confused.

Sam paused. "My jukebox has had a tendency to get stuck on that song. Therefore, none of us are huge fans—we like it—but we're scared it's going to get stuck again. Thank goodness if it does I have Norma Sue there who knows exactly how to fix it, just takes a lot of work. But still, there is always the possibility that it won't get unstuck. Or the possibility that it will just play it over and over again."

Lana laughed. "Well, I have to say I like it. I'm tempted, but I'm not going to go over there and dance with Esther Mae."

"Don't," App grunted. "That woman will come sit down in a minute. I think y'all are having a meeting."

"Yes, we are," Norma Sue declared. "Esther Mae, get over here. We've got a meeting to get ready for. I see everyone else getting out of their vehicles and coming across the road."

Esther Mae squealed with the song one more time and came rushing to the table. "I can't help it; I'm happy today. We're getting set up for the rodeo and sale this weekend and I'm just practicing for the dance afterwards." She sat by Lana and leaned into her. "Me and my sweet man are going to dance. And he can *dance,* so I have to practice."

"There's a dance after the rodeo?" Lana asked.

"Yes, ma'am. Always," Norma Sue said. "All the cowboys and cowgirls get out there and have fun. And us workers who worked our rears off to help sell the food and drinks need to have some fun too."

"So," Esther Mae elbowed her gently. "This will be your first fun event in Mule Hollow. You'll have to get out there and show us what you've got."

Lana swallowed hard. "I don't have anything. I've nerve pin—*never been* a dancer."

"Oh, come on now, everybody can dance. Especially if you've got the right partner." Esther Mae grinned. "And if he acts up you can pin him in the nerves, making him squeal."

Everyone laughed. "Esther Mae, you're a hoot."

"No, honey, you're the hoot. And that's better than a *poot*." She rolled her eyes and laughed. "But back to the subject at hand. My sweet Hank is the best in all the world. We just can't spend enough time together and that includes dancing. My spirits just rise, even after all these years, when he takes me in his arms and we dance."

Lana was dumbstruck. What would that be like? Her parents loved each other dearly but had never expressed love like this funny, exuberant woman. Lana would love to be that age and still be dancing on the dance floor.

She would have to actually get on the dance floor for that to be possible.

"Me and my Roy Don like to dance too," Norma

Sue added. "But I don't get out there and rock and roll like Esther Mae and Hank do. I like two steppin'. It's a fun dance even for a gal as big as me." She grinned. "You'll have to try it with the right partner."

Jeb's face filled her mind with the words and she wondered if he could dance. She wondered if he would be at the dance. She figured he would if that was where all the cowboys would be.

The door jingled and in walked Lacy, Izzy, and Sheri from the salon.

"Howdy," Lacy sang to the music. "Esther Mae, you're getting ready to dance. Norma Sue, you going to dance too?"

"No," Norma Sue said. "I'm worried that it isn't going to shut up and I'm going to have to fix it again."

Izzy grinned. "I like this song a lot."

"You haven't heard it as much as we have," Applegate boomed.

"You've got that right," Norma Sue agreed.

Lana looked at Norma Sue. "You sure are grumpy today."

"Awe heck. Yes, I'm grumpy. I didn't sleep well

last night. I've got a backache."

Izzy walked over to her. "I can help you."

"What do you mean you can help me?"

"Stand up and tell me where it's hurting."

Norma Sue stood up and Izzy walked behind her and poked her between the shoulder blades. "Right there?"

"Yes, how did you know?"

"The way you were sitting. Okay, stand there and wrap your arms across each other. Now just stand there and don't move."

Then Izzy wrapped her arms around the woman. Her arms barely fit around Norma, but she managed to get one hand locked on her other wrist. "Now I want you to take a deep breath and when I say breathe, I want you to let the air out."

"Why?"

"Just do what I say."

They watched as Norma Sue did exactly as Izzy said. Then Izzy leaned back squeezing hard, lifting Norma Sue off the ground a tad. Everyone heard a crack as Izzy put Norma Sue back down on her feet.

Lana wondered if Izzy had broken her back with the way she'd leaned back.

Izzy looked at all of them and laughed. "Why are y'all looking like that? Her back's better. Didn't you hear it?"

"We heard it alright," Esther Mae said. "But we thought it was your back because Norma Sue is a bit bigger than you—"

"Hush." Norma Sue laughed. "I've been working all my life and lifted a lot of weight around cows. Enjoying steaks and other things make me happy so I am what I am and proud of it. And my back feels a lot better."

Izzy was grinning. "I never told y'all that I can do more than just cut hair but don't want to. I saw Norma Sue in pain, so I helped. You don't do that unless you know how because you don't want to hurt someone."

"We won't try it." Lacy laughed. "If we did it wrong, we might break our own backs." Everyone laughed.

Lana just sat there, watching. Boy, she loved this place. Everyone had something fun, laughable…even her.

Maybe that was what drew her here. If she was going to have oddities, then she'd moved to the right place. As she contemplated this, Norma Sue slid back into the seat beside her and everyone else pulled chairs up around the table.

"Okay, everybody," Lacy said just as Molly Popp Jacobs walked in and pulled up a chair. Lana had seen most of the ladies at church, but she was still learning names, like Dottie, the director of No Place Like Home.

The ladies started talking about what they were going to bring to the concession stand and Lana was glad she was there and able to work. The more they talked, the more excited she got. She hadn't been to a rodeo in a very long time. And then she thought of Jeb.

Would he be there?

Would he compete—or did he even know how to rodeo? Maybe he would sing. She'd loved his singing from the show that night and would love to hear him sing again.

She hadn't talked to him in so long. She'd just seen him at a distance, as if he was purposely staying away.

She hated that. But at a dance it might be…what was she thinking? Did she want to dance with the cowboy?

At that moment the jukebox switched songs and Elvis Presley's *"You Ain't Nothing But A Hound Dog"* rang out in the room.

Lana chuckled to herself. She felt like a hound dog, thinking about Jeb more than she wanted to, as if her brain couldn't get enough of him.

"Now we're playing some music," Esther Mae squealed, and Lana laughed.

And oh, how she needed that laugh.

And that *man.*

And *that* thought struck her like lightning.

CHAPTER THIRTEEN

"So, I'll be ready to come back to the show after this next weekend," Ross said as he rode with Jeb to check on the cattle branding. They had hired extra men to help round them up and brand them. Many of Ross's friends also came to help because they knew he couldn't do it yet.

"That's good. Your wife will be glad to have you back."

He grinned. "Yep, but then remember I told you we were having a baby—it's official. Doc says he's doing well so we're about to announce it."

"Congratulations."

Ross smiled. "Thanks. God is good. Sugar Rae is pregnant, meaning I'm going to be a daddy."

Jeb took his foot off the gas and stared at his cousin, suddenly not sure where the conversation was going now. "I bet Sugar Rae is ecstatic."

"She is. That woman is going to be a fantastic mom and she's happy it's ours. But like I said, we're going to have more than one. We're blessed with this pregnancy, but we are going to fill this ranch up with at least four kids. She's going to tell the group soon, but not yet. We're giving everything a little more time. But I wanted you to know. We talked about it and like I said, I'm going to back away. I've got a baby coming and more will come. That means I'm throwing all my weight into my ranch, building it up and making it what I dreamed it to be. Sugar loves the stage but knows she's going to love her children more, so she's going to be looking for a replacement in the show and go at it as a manager and not the actress."

"That's all fantastic." They were done performing.

"We think so. But before she starts looking, we want to make sure you don't want the spot. You would have a say in the show, what you want to perform."

Did he want the spot? The idea hadn't settled well

before but now, for some reason, he'd been looking forward to the next show. He'd told himself it was because it would be his last, but now… He needed to think.

A couple of shows a month, or even two weekends out of a month, wasn't rough. He knew he was good, no bragging involved. But was he enjoying it because he loved it or just because it wasn't two shows a day every day?

"No need to answer right away, we just wanted to put it out there for you," Ross interrupted his thoughts.

"Okay, thanks. I need to think about it."

"That's a good sign. No pressure though. This is your choice."

As they watched the cowboys branding the cattle, Jeb's mind was on what his cousin had just offered him.

He would have a say in the show. He'd have the choice of what he wanted to sing and to say.

It was the first time he had that as an option.

Jeb found all the ranching and cattle work fascinating and wanted to be a rancher like Ross.

Did he want to keep singing as well? On his own

terms? His own show? His choices?

By the time they headed back to the house, Ross was hurting but not saying so. "I'll be glad when that's gone and you're back to normal," said Jeb.

Ross grinned. "That will be soon. Thanks for standing in at the show. If you decide you want to take the show, the pay will be a partnership if you want. It's up to you."

"Thanks. I'll let you know."

* * *

By late afternoon on Saturday, Lana was excited about the rodeo. Just being involved was a great feeling. Since coming to Mule Hollow, she'd been involved but hadn't felt like she was all in. She worked in the real estate office but didn't see that many people. She'd go to Sam's and see Applegate and Stanley and whoever else might be there. And sometimes she'd sit with the Posse. She really enjoyed them.

It was odd because, at first, she thought they were targeting her and trying to get her and Jeb together. But they'd backed off. She was pretty sure it had to do with everyone knowing she was recovering from—the name of her illness didn't come to her. It was a hard name to remember, and since it caused this, she didn't feel bad about forgetting it.

She'd like to forget it completely and be back to normal, but she'd learned to live with it. Maybe the Posse backing off and knowing she wasn't a target anymore had helped her. She enjoyed sitting with them and when their chats got funny. But she felt a little frustrated thinking about it. They tried to fix everyone up. But with her, they'd—what? Backed down. They were treating her like she was a delicate piece of tissue paper.

Did she want them to get involved? What was she thinking? Did she want to be a match made in Mule Hollow?

Lana drove her Jeep to Clint and Lacy's ranch. It was really nice and mighty big. The ranch had to be worth a lot but that didn't keep Lacy from working three days a week. That lady loved her work and her clients. But she loved her kids too. Lacy loved everything. It was a great way to be—happy and relaxed and fulfilled. And she let everyone know it.

Lana loved her life too. She was thrilled to still have it to enjoy. But in the last few weeks, especially this last week, she had sensed that something was missing. Her words and her thoughts were better but still off in the most unexpected places. But she wasn't stressing over it. Everyone took her the way she was. They had patience and fun when she struggled to get the right word or blurted out a completely off the wall word.

She was smiling, thinking about those times when she stopped her Jeep in the middle of the drive. Not far away, she saw Jeb getting out of his truck. Seeing him told her the truth: she'd missed him.

He'd stayed away, given her room, and she'd let him. Heart thundering, she wanted…what?

She wanted to see him more. She'd enjoyed her first week so much. Why? Because she'd enjoyed being with him. She'd told him everything about her illness and recovery before telling anyone.

He must have recognized the sound of her Jeep engine. He stopped where he was and looked down the long row of cars to where she sat in her Jeep just looking at him. He stood there unmoving looking at her.

He started walking her way when a car pulled in behind her and she had to move forward. He stopped where he was and pointed to the empty parking space next to his truck. She pulled in and shut off her engine as he walked around to where she sat. She didn't get out. She just sat there, heart pounding with a sporadic pulse as he stopped beside her seat.

He put his left hand on the top of her windshield and his right hand on the Jeep's seat. He was so close she could smell his aftershave, its tangy and clean aroma filling her senses.

"How are you?" he asked.

She looked at him. "I'm doing good. I'm good. I'm—" *saying I'm, I'm, I'm,* she thought. If she was going to say anything, she needed to get her words straight, but with him standing so close…almost like an embrace without touching her. She had an erratic heartbeat and felt what? Tempted. Tempted to lean forward and get him to come a little closer. After all he was already leaning forward.

She took a deep breath and looked at him instead. "I'm not stumbling over my words as much. As you can tell, it still happens. But," she smiled, "everyone is so supportive. And I've learned just to laugh and go on. You know we talked about that, and it helped me. But I…" She couldn't finish. She got scared. All she could think about was how she had flung her arms around him after they'd fallen down that ravine. She was the one who kissed him first. And he'd kissed back.

Her brain had gone blank looking at him with that serious look in his eyes. A sizzling feeling was erupting inside her. In all that she'd been through, she knew she wasn't dead when she was near this man.

"It's good to see you," she finished.

His gaze faltered, then held hers. "I've missed you." He removed his arms and hands from her Jeep and stepped back. "So, you're here to watch the rodeo?"

"From the concession stand." She grinned. "If there's a view from there. I'm counting the money."

"You'll have a view. Are you coming to the dance?"

"I am. Not that I'm a dancer. But I enjoy the music

and watching everyone." She got out of the Jeep, heart continuing to race. "Do you dance?"

"Sometimes."

As they walked toward the arena, she realized that she didn't want to walk away from him but she had to. "I guess I'll see you later."

"Save a dance for me," he said when the concession stand came into view.

She paused, "Okay." She walked toward the concession stand knowing her day had just gotten better. When she looked over her shoulder and found him watching her, she smiled as her heart continued to flutter.

She hoped if he asked her to dance that she could get out there and do it without stumbling over her feet.

* * *

He had acted on impulse when he saw her. Closing in around her as she sat in her Jeep, eye to eye with him, and only inches away had been a crazy moment he wouldn't take back. He'd missed her.

Jeb enjoyed watching the rodeo. He stood near the chutes with some of his new friends. Luc Asher was a horse trainer Jeb had met when he arrived. He was about his age and really great at training horses. He was going to start teaching Jeb what he did and he was looking forward to it.

However, his mind went to Lana. He wanted to talk to her, dance with her, and see if there was any chance of anything happening between them. He'd kept busy but she was always on his mind. Earlier there had been a look in her eyes that pulled at him. Told him maybe tonight would be the night to take a step closer and a dance might be the perfect way.

"Hey, cowboy," he turned at the sing-song voice of Lacy Brown Matlock. Her name, like her voice, went together as it played together in an unusual way.

"Hey, Lacy, how are you?"

"I'm good. Great. I've been getting the concession stand filled with great things to buy. All the money is going to go to No Place Like Home."

"That's great."

"I'm hoping everyone buys something so we'll sell

out. If you don't mind, please remind anyone you talk to about it. And come on over and grab something yourself."

"Sure. I'll do that."

"Lana will be taking the money. She's good at counting money. Did you know that?"

"She'll be good; she knows how to smile. And that sometimes gets people to come back for more."

Lacy hitched a brow. "You're right. I made a good choice then. You know that infection she had is so odd. But she's improved so much. She makes mistakes with her words sometimes, but not like she was doing. Have you noticed?"

"I haven't talked to her in a while. Tonight was the first time in a couple of weeks. She was still getting her words wrong then."

"She still is, just not so much. But I think she's missing something else."

"What?"

"You."

He stared at Lacy. "Me. Why do you say that?"

Lacy shrugged. "I just watch and have noticed that

she hasn't said much about you lately. But she also hasn't taken that Jeep of hers out on a drive. And you know me and my pink Caddy like to ride. So, I'm wondering if some riding around would be good for her."

What was Lacy implying?"

"She did tell me about y'all falling down a ravine. The Posse and me think something changed in her after that. Did she hit her head? We know you took a fall too."

"No, she didn't hit her head." He remembered the terrified feeling he had when he saw her disappear over the edge of that ravine. He knew nothing had ever affected him the way that moment had. The kiss after he dove after her and joined her in the mud was a memory of another form that he couldn't forget. He went to bed thinking about it and woke up still thinking about it. He knew he would want that moment back every day of his life.

"I lost you to a deep thought," Lacy said. "Thinking about Lana?"

Lacy had a way, like she could look inside his head and his heart. "I am. I can't get her off my mind."

That got him a wide smile and her blue eyes lit up. "Then you need to do something about that. I can tell you that it is driving the Posse crazy not being able to set you two up. They don't know when the time would be right for Lana. So, they've backed off. But me, well I saw you two when you got here—staring at each other. There is something brewing between you two and you need to act. She needs you."

She needed him. He wasn't so sure about that, but he knew without a doubt that he needed her and wanted her in his life.

"Dance with her tonight and don't fight it. Let it happen naturally. Don't turn it away."

"But I don't want to hurt her."

Lacy smiled. "That lady is one tough cookie. So, don't give up."

She walked away, leaving Jeb speechless.

Could he do what Lacy asked?

CHAPTER FOURTEEN

"How are you feeling?" Adela asked softly, standing beside Lana in the refreshment stand.

"Fine," Lana responded. She had been standing for two hours counting money and smiling as she gave all the wonderful people their change.

"Are you sure? You still need to rest, and you've been busy."

Lana took a moment and knew Adela was right—oh, how she wanted to be back to normal. But she would be, it was just going to take time. Yes, her brain might never get back to being normal but she was getting back in shape. Now, she considered how standing and counting money worked her mentally and physically—

though she was about to start pushing herself on the physical exercise.

Seven months and she still had weaknesses which irritated her, but she could fix that. "Y'all need me," she said, knowing good and well what Adela was going to say.

Adela smiled and covered Lana's hands with her left hand. "I'll take it from here. I've just been back there stirring cheese dip in the Crock-Pots, so my mind is still fresh. Go take a little time and enjoy sitting in the stands so you'll be ready to dance in a bit."

Well, she hadn't known exactly what the sweet lady was going to say but she did want to enjoy watching everyone dance later tonight.

Lacy walked into the booth after running an errand. "Go sit down and enjoy the show. The last thing we want is to wear you out, girlfriend."

"Okay, but I really enjoyed helping."

"Honey," Esther Mae declared. "You are not being put out to pasture. We will welcome you to more things than you might have ever imagined. We're just making sure you get well so we can use you some more." She hooted with laughter and Lana did too.

Laughing and feeling good, Lana waved goodbye and walked out into the area between the stadium seats.

"The seats are better if you go to the right," Lacy called and gave her a smile.

Lana went right. She walked along the rock walkway running at the base of the steps and seats. Before she reached the handrail and steps to walk up to find a seat, she saw Jeb standing a few feet further down the walkway. She halted in her tracks. He was watching Bob on his horse, weaving one way then the other as the horse and the calf played dodgeball—no ball allowed. It looked like a horse and a cow dancing, but her gaze was locked on the handsome cowboy.

Her insides quivered as she stepped toward him and propped her elbows on the rail beside him. "Looks like they're dancing."

His hat almost flew off as he turned his head so quickly to look at her. "Lana." His lips curled upward and so did hers. "Good to see you."

"Good to see you," she said, breathless as her insides sizzled as his smile grew. Oh, she had missed his smile. "Have you been fixin' fences this week?"

"I have."

"I hope it's going well."

"It is. No cliffs to fall down."

"Me not there to find it."

"No, if you were there, you couldn't find them. That fence is fixed. Next week there is another show at the barn," he said, changing the subject.

"Mind if I come watch?"

"No, actually, I was going to come ask you if you'd come. I'd love for you to come watch it and give me your opinion. I am going to change it up a bit. I have a lot on my mind."

"Really, what's on your mind? Why are you changing things?"

He looked at her, something going on behind those golden eyes of his. Eyes she'd missed.

"I can't say a lot, but I have the opportunity to start performing on a regular show schedule. My cousin and his wife are going to back off and need someone to replace them…I've had a lot on my mind about it."

"You mean you might use that amazing voice of

yours for every show?" It was something she could listen to always.

"So, you like my voice?"

Her heart pounded once more. "I do. I don't know how anyone could not love your voice. It's a gift from God."

"Thank you." His golden eyes glittered in the stadium lights from above them. Her insides tickled at the look. "I got burnt out and wanted something different. But then Ross asked me if I wanted to take the lead position, and I can't get it off my mind. This is different. It's all me, my choices, my story."

She wanted to reach out and touch his arm but she didn't. "That's something new for you. Would you still be able to ranch?"

"Yes, the show would be part of my life but not all of it. I'd have room for everything else I've been dreaming of."

Her pulse blew up at the way his eyes focused on her. "That's good," she managed.

"Are you taking a break from the concession stand?" he asked.

Change of topic, smart move away from where they'd been going. "I am. Adela took my place, suggesting I needed to rest before the big dance. And she was right. Adela is always right."

He grinned widely. "That's what I hear. I'm glad she realized you needed a break. I read that rest was needed for your recovery."

He'd been studying her illness. That warmed her heart. "Yes, that's true. But I'm so ready to be back to normal. They say it's coming."

"And so it shall. Come on, let's go on up and sit so you can relax." He stepped to the steps and held out his hand. "I'll hold on to you this time, just in case—" He stopped talking. "Well, I'm sure you'd make it up on your own."

Before he finished, she'd slipped her hand in his. He had given her a reason to hold his hand, feel his touch and she knew she wasn't letting anything get in the way of that. His hand was warm, electrifying. Wonderful.

As if he felt it too, his fingers tightened around hers in an easy but strong hold. They started up the stairs hand in hand. Everyone on either side could see them holding hands as they made their way up the steps. She loved it and the fact that her hand in his felt right.

The area at the top bleacher was empty and Lana liked that it was only the two of them there at the top of the stands. She felt in that moment, at the top of the world.

He sat down and kept her hand in his as she sat down beside him. Their legs touched and she didn't move away. Breathless—not from the walk but from Jeb's nearness, Lana focused on Bob on the cutting horse. "He's good."

"Very good. Bob used to be one of the best clowns around."

"A clown?"

He looked at her and smiled. "He was a rodeo clown, also known as a rodeo bullfighter. It takes a lot of talent, agility, and energy to be a bullfighter in a rodeo, especially a championship bullfighter like he was. It's funny that they dress up like clowns for entertainment, but they are the toughest dudes out there in a rodeo."

"I remember being at a rodeo with my mom and dad. I thought the clown was so funny. He had a dog with him and a big old tub he'd put between him and the bull sometimes. He could dodge the bull's horns. It's a workout and a lifesaver to the congestion—contestants."

"Exactly. Now he competes with his own horses and owns his own herds of cattle. No clowns allowed." He grinned and his hand tightened on hers in a gentle pressure.

She smiled back at him and happily left her hand in his as the night continued. She just enjoyed being near him.

"How are you doing?" he asked a little later as the rodeo was nearing its end.

"Good. Adela was right; I needed to rest."

"I'm glad she sent you to the stands."

"She did, but Lacy told me which direction to go for a seat."

"Lacy. She's like a bullfighter."

Lana looked at him. "How's that?"

He grinned. "They make moves that get the bull to

move the direction they want the bull to go. In your case, she made the move, assuming that would send you my way. She and I had just had a conversation before you came my way."

"So, you think…"

"I think she's one smart clown and sent you my way like the leader of the Posse that she is."

"Oh," she gasped, then smiled. "And I fell for it."

"I'm glad you did."

They locked gazes. Her heart went into bull bucking mode and she held on, determined to hold on and not need the services of a bullfighter.

* * *

The rodeo ended and Jeb was thrilled that Lana had let him hold her hand all night. But he didn't want to crowd her. He'd initially taken her hand because he wanted to and because he wasn't going to let her walk up the stairs without his help. Just in case she needed him.

Needed him. That was the way it started out, but he knew all the way to the center of his soul that *he* needed her. There had been no denying it.

But he didn't want to press his luck so when they were back on steady ground, he released her hand. "Can I walk you to the dance area?"

"Sure, since I'm not sure where it is." She looked around the crowd.

"Walk this way," he said and motioned for her to walk beside him.

Along the way they stopped and talked with different friends of his and hers. It felt right, her by his side and him by her side.

He wanted this. Wanted her. Wanted a life they could create together with God at the center. The One who'd put them together.

By the time they reached the area past the barns, which was lit up with lights strung like Christmas over the dance floor, some of the cowboys from the show were already playing music. Jeb knew it was going to be a great dance.

If he got Lana out on the dance floor even one time, it would be an awesome dance.

"Lookin' good, you two," Esther Mae called,

grinning big as she and Hank spun by on the dance floor. "Come on out here."

He grinned. "That lady can dance."

"She loves it."

The music was a slow song, a beautiful song, a song that knocked him in the heart. The cowboys were playing, "You Had Me From Hello". The moment he'd slammed on his brakes and saw her standing in the middle of Main Street, nothing in his life had been the same. He held his hand out. "Dance with me?" he asked.

Her gaze locked on his hand and then she nodded and placed her hand once more in his, as he led her out onto the dance floor this time. No danger for anything but his heart on this trip.

He turned and gently took her in his arms.

"Remember, I'm not that good—" She trailed off, her voice shaky.

"Just follow my lead and if not, that's okay—all I want is to hold you in my arms and dance." And they did. Moving together, her eyes locked with his, her feet moved with his...like it was meant to be, they danced.

He prayed it wasn't all in his head and that she felt

what he felt. For now, he took what she gave him, and it was a dance he'd never forget. Just like every other moment they'd spent together. God was good in mysterious ways.

And he liked it.

As the song played, she finally, for all to see, laid her forehead against his shoulder and he knew he never wanted to let her go.

And as the next song began it was as if it had been picked for them, because "Forever and For Always" played and he knew that was what he wanted with Lana. Forever and for always.

* * *

Lana felt as if she was floating as she awoke the next morning. Her dancing with Jeb had been unbelievable. And she wanted to dance with him forever, but could she risk letting herself feel this way?

It was Sunday morning, and she was going to church, but she wanted to walk the river trail before she dressed for service. It was barely six so that gave her time. Lana dressed in jeans, hiking boots, and a t-shirt. When she arrived, she parked her Jeep and took her bottle of water, and went down the trail to the river's edge. Oh, how she loved this spot. There was peace— she smiled as the song "Peace Like a River" flowed through her. After walking the trail a bit, she sat on the edge where her feet were on one trail and her rear rested on another. Cattle loved traveling various trails and this was the perfect place for her to relax.

Her world had been turned upside down, and that had brought her to this spot this morning. Last night she'd known that she was in love with the man she'd met in the first moments she'd driven into Mule Hollow. But was she rushing things?

Was her mind well enough to see if what she felt in his arms last night was what she hoped and prayed it would be?

She lowered her head and said a prayer for God to guide her. When she lifted her head and opened her eyes, Jeb stood on the trail looking straight at her.

"Jeb."

He smiled. "Lana. You're making my heart sing

right now."

"Right back at you."

He stepped her way. "I had to come here in hopes of at least feeling your presence here from the last time you were here. And I was going to pray for guidance."

She stepped toward him. "Guidance?"

"In this relationship I want with you, *Lana*. I've never wanted anything more than what I want to have and build with you. A life for both of us."

Her lips spread into a wide smile. "That's why I'm here…"

Unable to stop, she stepped toward him as he drew close to her. He pulled her close and his lips came down on hers. They kissed a kiss full of hope and…love. She loved this man. This man who'd come into her life and awakened something in her heart that her wobbly brain needed. Unable to stop herself, she said the words. "Jeb, I love you."

He pulled back and looked at her. "And if my words before weren't clear, maybe my words need working on. Honey, I love you too, more than anything I could have ever imagined or dreamed of before you walked into my life."

Her lips trembled and her eyes sparkled with joy. Hugging her close they stood there by the river, the sound of the moving water and the soft singing of the birds played their love song and peace and hope embraced them.

"Just remember I didn't and don't want to take this too fast," he said. "But it's been a runaway crash waiting to happen in my heart since that sunrise morning when I first saw you."

"Me too, though I tried not to go too fast."

"I want to help you heal to the best of your ability and help you use what God's given to you to help others. I want to be with you now and love every minute with you." He went down on his knee, holding her hand. "Lana, will you let me travel this road of recovery with you? Our life together will be full of love, laughter, and forever, will you marry me?"

Tears welled in her eyes, and she nodded. "I will."

He was up in a second and she was in his arms as he hugged her tight.

"Lana, we're going to have a wonderful life

together."

She leaned her head against his shoulder and nodded. "Yes, we are. It's already made it to wonderful. Now onward to forever." She lifted herself on her tiptoes and met his lips…and this kiss locked them into a future they would make together.

Good words, mixed-up words, funny words, but all full of love and the knowledge that they'd been given a gift that they were not going to ever take for granted. Oh, how good God was…they had a future they'd never imagined. And love that would never end.

Looking up at Jeb, she grinned. "Oh, what a love story I'm going to write. And maybe, a barn shoe— *show* for the man I love to hear sing."

"Honey, shoe or show I'm in all the way."

Looking at each other their grins grew and then they laughed…let the fun begin.

And a happily-ever-after it was right then and there on the score—the *shore* of the flowing river of love that for them would never end…life was a gift and she was going to enjoy it forever more with this loving, giving, amazing man of her heart.

About the Author

Debra Clopton is a USA Today bestselling & International bestselling author who has sold over 3.5 million books. She has published over 81 books under her name and her pen name of Hope Moore.

Under both names she writes clean & wholesome and inspirational, small town romances, especially with cowboys but also loves to sweep readers away with romances set on beautiful beaches surrounded by topaz water and romantic sunsets.

Her books now sell worldwide and are regulars on the Bestseller list in the United States and around the world. Debra is a multiple award-winning author, but of all her awards, it is her reader's praise she values most. If she can make someone smile and forget their worries for a few hours (or days when binge reading one of her series) then she's done her job and her heart is happy. She really loves hearing she kept a reader from doing the dishes or sleeping!

A sixth-generation Texan, Debra lives on a ranch in Texas with her husband surrounded by cattle, deer, very busy squirrels and hole digging wild hogs. She enjoys traveling and spending time with her family.

Visit Debra's website and sign up for her newsletter for updates at: www.debraclopton.com

Check out her Facebook at: www.facebook.com/debra.clopton.5

Follow her on Instagram at: debraclopton_author

or contact her at debraclopton@ymail.com

www.ingramcontent.com/pod-product-compliance
Lightning Source LLC
Chambersburg PA
CBHW070649100726
47907CB00007B/2153